Universal Television and
Amblin Entertainment present

The Novel by

Diane Duane and
Peter Morwood

based upon the teleplay by Rockne S. O'Bannon
and Tommy Thompson
Story by Rockne S. O'Bannon

MILLENNIUM
An Orion Book
LONDON

This edition first published
in Great Britain in 1993 by
Millennium
An imprint of Orion Books Ltd
Orion House, 5 Upper St Martin's Lane
London WC2H 9EA

A CIP catalogue record for this book is available
from the British Library

ISBN: (Csd) 1 85798 183 9

Millennium
Book Thirty One

Filmset by Selwood Systems, Midsomer Norton
Printed and bound in Great Britain by
Butler & Tanner Ltd, Frome, Somerset

ONE

It is common knowledge to everyone, mariner or not, that the sea can get damnably rough and dangerous when a storm blows up. But it takes a *sub*mariner to know how calm that same stormy sea can be, once you drop below the wind-whipped surface and down into the peaceful depths.

There are mineral mining fields scattered all across the seabeds of every ocean, and those which border the Livingston Trench lie two hundred and fifty fathoms down … fifteen hundred feet below the waves. It can be a very peaceful place indeed: calm, still, dark – and far enough from the concerns of the world and its industrial confederations to let a man get on with scratching a more or less honest living.

Although that honesty depends a great deal on whether he stays where he belongs, and doesn't wander where he shouldn't. In the second decade of the Twenty-first Century, so much money is being made from the mining of the ocean floor that the depths have ceased to be peaceful. Territorial borders can be just as sensitive beneath the sea as anywhere on land.

And just as heavily defended ...

*

Bobby MacLaine crouched over the controls of his pickup truck. His hands were on its control yoke, not lightly, but in a white-knuckled grip so tight that his fingers should have left grooves in the worn plastic bars. Even though it was already running flat out, Bobby needed to squeeze a couple of extra knots out of the truck's hydrojet propulsion system. He would have scrambled out of his seat and kicked the laboring motor if that would have done any good, but from the howling noises it had been making this past five minutes, he already knew that he was getting the best the elderly unit was able to give. And even that might not be enough.

The truck – a cargo flatbed with a pressurized spherical cab stuck on the front like a Tinker-toy afterthought – had been designed for deep sea transport work. It had *not* been designed with high-speed chases in mind. Not that twenty knots was high-speed in anybody's language, but it would be more than fast enough if Bobby slapped cab-first into a rock outcrop. At this depth, the pressure pod would crack like an eggshell, and it would all be over in a crushed split-second. If the water came slamming in, he wouldn't even live long enough to drown. Bobby was twenty-two years old, and he didn't want to die. Least of all that way. Even though it might be less painful and certainly quicker than being caught by –

– Bobby glanced at the mirrors and the video repeater

that covered the truck's rear quarter, and swallowed nervously. There was nothing yet, even though that didn't mean a thing. If they were running on sonar with their lights doused, they could be right on top of him before he saw anything. Earl's truck had the sonar emitter required by the traffic-safety regulations, but it was strictly directional, and that direction was the one in which the truck was travelling. Nobody had ever bothered with a passive all-round pickup. Nobody had ever seen the need for one. Until now.

Bobby shoved his scruffy baseball cap back on his head and wiped sweat from his face with the sleeve of an equally scruffy flannel shirt, then grabbed the radio mike from its cradle and keyed a home channel.

'Reef runner to Home Plate ...!' There was no response except for the disinterested hiss of static and the feedback hum of the truck's own electrics. 'Come in, Home Plate! –' He stared nervously at the mike and keyed it off, then on again. Still no reply, except the frying-fat noise of interference.

Or could it be jamming?

No ... nobody down here had any of that stuff. At least, nobody he knew about. But had *they*? He glanced at the rearviews again, and felt his shirt beginning to stick to his back. 'Come on,' he pleaded, 'come on, pick it up –!'

The answering voice spoke so very suddenly that though he had desperately wanted to hear it, the sound still made him jump. *'Home Plate to Reef Runner – go ahead –'*

'Jenny!' he cried, 'it's Bobby!'

'Where the hell have you been?' He could hear the concern in her voice, but it was edged with the weary anger and impatience Bobby had heard often enough before when

one of his stunts backfired. That was only to be expected – except that this time Jenny didn't know just how serious the backfire had been.

No matter that she couldn't see the gesture, Bobby shook his head desperately. The explanations and accusations would have to wait until later, or he might not *have* a later ... 'Never mind! Just open up the main airlock quick! I'm comin' in – and I've got company!'

There was no reply except for the click as she closed the mike at her end, and then the feedback on the open channel changed from a hum to a deep, ominous drone like the warning sound of a swarm of hornets. Bobby swallowed. No single motor could generate that amount of interference, no matter how hard it was being worked. There was more company than he had expected. He looked at the rearview again, and swore under his breath as a yellow glow began to leave flare-tracks across the screen.

The glow brightened, separated, became two sources, and kept on coming.

'Uh-oh, Bobby,' he mumbled to himself, grateful for any sympathetic voice, even if only his own. 'Look sharp ...'

The pursuing trucks drew closer, and he could tell from its quad light array that one of them was the big three-pod semi variant. That meant it had a heavy-duty hydrojet impeller: more speed if it was unloaded, as it surely was, and more weight if its driver tried to ram him – as he surely would, if he could overhaul Bobby's frantically-racing pickup. Collisions were the sort of accidents easily explained, because they happened frequently enough in the often-murky water of the mining fields, despite lights and sonar. But because of the deceleration jets automatically cut in by a proximity echo return, they were not usually fatal.

Not usually.

Bobby MacLaine knew well enough that if it ever took place, his collision *would* be fatal. Even if they had to hit him a dozen times to make sure of it. He knew. He had made them mad enough. Then he saw the harsh blue light of the Home Plate beacon, and grinned in relief.

Blink-blink. Blink. Blink. Blink-blink.

Five hundred yards away the beacon paused, then repeated its patterned signal. Bobby twisted the truck's control yoke that necessary few degrees to bring him into line for the MacLaine outpost's airlock approach. The vehicle yawed ominously as his hastily-loaded cargo of ore samples lurched across the cargo bed, then corrected as he fed in a couple of squirts from the manoeuvering thrusters. Nearly home, and he wasn't dead in the water yet.

There had still been no further online response from Jenny, probably in case someone was listening in on the same channel, but the ID beacon told him that she was doing the only thing she could. Outpost beacons normally ran white, but the shift to blue meant that the main airlock was cycling open. As he squinted through the undersea gloom, trying to filter out the glow of his own dashboard instruments, he could actually see the massive doors sliding back. All he had to do now was reach them before the two pursuing trucks reached *him* ...

That was when the pickup's hydrojet unit coughed, then began to make a grinding noise Bobby had never heard before. And he never wanted to hear it again, because it sounded like a garbage disposal digesting broken glass. He didn't need to look at the thrust readout to know that the little truck was losing way. He *felt* it. The entire vehicle had faltered as though the water surrounding it had suddenly gone thick, and though the shudder of deceleration had lasted only for an instant before the impeller spooled up again, that instant was long enough for the lights in the rearview screen to come surging closer.

'C'mon, sweet thing,' he crooned, fighting down a renewed desire to kick the engine, and deciding against even swearing at it. 'C'mon. You can do it ...'

As if spurred on to greater effort by the encouragement, the waterjet whined thinly and increased its output by another few revs. Not enough for the pursuing trucks to fall back, but at least sufficient to keep them where they were.

Then the airlock doors stopped momentarily, and just before they started to move again, the beacon light turned red. It confirmed what his eyes had already told him. The airlock was no longer opening, but closing ...

Bobby's speeding pickup was two hundred yards away, and closing ...

The hornets on his tail were a hundred yards behind, and closing ...

Bobby MacLaine licked his lips, and took a deep breath that he knew might soon be crushed out of him by the weight of two hundred atmospheres of water. Rather than running the risk of letting the pursuing trucks follow him into the airlock, Jenny was putting her faith in his ability as a waterjet jockey. It was a faith that might get him killed if she was wrong; but if the men in the trucks behind him got into the outpost, that might get them *both* killed. This was a notoriously rough territory, and accidents could happen to a pressure-dome just as easily as to a truck ...

Bobby grinned nervously at his own reflection; then he eased off on the pickup's control yoke, stabilized it with the merest fingertip pressure – and aimed the little craft straight for the gap between the doors.

Too narrow! screamed a panicked voice at the back of his mind. *You're gonna smash for sure!* He tried to ignore it. He had done this before – once – and both Earl and Jenny had given him an epic bawling-out. Why was doing it again, and with permission this time, making him so scared? There wasn't any difference. Except that if he chickened out, there was nowhere else for him to go. The other trucks would catch him, and … Bobby stamped on the rest of the thought.

One hundred yards, and closing …

Closing at twenty knots. More than enough to do the business if he fumbled it. At two hundred atmospheres he would barely live long enough to feel the consequences of an error if his cab cracked open. The outer airlock doors were sliding shut like the jaws of a Great White Shark that Bobby had seen once on an EarthNet educational vid. In slo-mo. But without teeth. These didn't need teeth. Even without its hydraulic motivators, each valve weighed seventeen tons, and whether they crunched into him or he crunched into them would make very little difference.

Except that it wasn't slo-mo. They were moving in real time, and so was he. 'Here we go, Bobby boy,' he whispered to himself and the pickup as he dove toward the doors. 'Think thin … think thin –!' but now, finally, Bobby could see that he had them beaten.

The pickup shot into the airlock so close and so fast that its pressure-wave produced a momentary rumble of cavitation from the steel lips of the doors. They were no more than eight inches away on either side, but even eight inches of clearance was enough. Bobby felt and heard the rumble, saw the rearview screen briefly silvered with swirling skeins of bubbles squeezed from the water by the pickup's passage – and saw his pursuers veer frantically aside to avoid the twin slabs of metal that were already too narrow for them to pass.

He started to laugh, the wild laughter of released tension, and was still laughing when the sonar emitter picked up the back of the outpost's airlock bay and shrieked a collision warning. Its blast of braking thrust shook the pickup like a rat in a terrier's teeth and sent him sliding out of his seat, but even after his butt hit the floor, he was still laughing.

The laughing was under control when he came into the outpost's control room, even though the grinning was not. Neither was the shaking of his hands, but as usual he wouldn't have admitted that. It was a place like his clothes, like his pickup, like everything here; a little scuffed, a little scruffy, but lovingly maintained and completely functional. He would never have said so aloud, and might have gotten his ears boxed if he had, but Earl and Jenny were all of a piece with the place where they lived.

*

Jenny was tucked into the outpost's communications bay, leaning over its systems panel as though it was an antique foot-treadle sewing machine. She was a woman somewhere in her forties, with a handsome, strong-featured face that concealed most of the traces of a hard life, and her plaid flannel shirt and blue jeans were a memory of an older time, but the way she wore her hair caught up in a severe bun was an echo of a time still farther back in history. A time when tough middle-aged ladies like her wore poke bonnets, and crouched in the shelter of horse-drawn wagons while they loaded rifles as long as their skirts to help keep the bad guys at bay. The wagons might not be horse-drawn any more, but the frontiers were just as harsh.

And the bad guys just as bad.

Jenny wasn't wearing a bonnet, just the fiber-optic headset that linked her to the outpost's comms bay, but her expression was as grave as though an entire gang of rustlers was pouring down on the homestead. As she looked up from the console, Bobby waved at her, not caring that the gesture was ignored, then sagged elaborately against a bulkhead.

'Wooo-hee!' He pulled off his baseball cap and fanned himself with it. 'I thought those hornets had me for sure!'

Jenny gave him a quick sideways glance and a nod of acknowledgment, then turned her attention back to the comms panel. She toggled a band-width switch and fine-tuned the receiver, frowning as she listened to the headset, her ears filtering out anything else he might have said with the ease of long practice as she hunted for coherence through the squeals of static and the chatter of too many voices on the same wavelength. Whether the attitude was deliberate because of what he had been doing, or accidental because of her own preoccupation, the effect was the same. It was as if Bobby didn't exist, and it served to calm his forced exuberance as effectively as a bucket of cold water. Dusting himself down, he replaced his cap then wandered over to her.

'Jenny, your timing with the airlock doors was just –'

9

'Sshhh!'

The way she shook him off shut Bobby up as sharply as if she had slapped his face and Jenny might have felt sorry for him. Or then again, maybe not. Enough had changed in the past few hours that she was no longer the easygoing woman he had left behind. Jenny knew there was a severity about her that he hadn't seen before; and hidden behind it, a fear and a helplessness that spread like a chill in the air.

The Winchesters were down to a handful of shells apiece, and the rustlers were still coming ...

She switched the headset's mike to standby and pushed it to one side, then kicked her chair back from the comms bay and spun it slowly around to better stare at him. He didn't stare back, and that was enough to make Jenny's lips compress into a thin, worried line. All right, not rustlers then. Claim-jumpers. And all of a sudden there was a doubt in her mind about whether *they* were really the bad guys after all. Because if they weren't, who was? Knowing Bobby only too well, she had her suspicions about that.

'You were prospecting over the territorial line, weren't ya?'

'No way!' Bobby said – but at the same time, he stared at the control panels and wouldn't meet her eyes. It told her the truth she had already guessed, even before he looked up again, and said, 'Well ... maybe a little ...' Then as usual he suddenly got all aggressively defensive about it, in the way Jenny had seen a thousand times before. 'But, hell, everybody does it!'

If everybody warmed their backsides by sitting in a fire, would you do that as well? thought Jenny, and grimaced sourly as she realized he probably would. There was no point in saying anything; over the past few years it had all been said before, too many times, and each time with less and less effect. Furious, she shook her head and rather than wasting any more time trying to deal with him, went back to scanning the frequencies. At once, and with a rising sense of unease, she noticed that in just the few seconds she'd been off-line, the babble of transmissions had doubled. Bobby must have read something of that concern on her face, because his own expression shifted slowly from penitent truculence. For the first time since he had stepped into the outpost he began to look worried, and Jenny had an ugly feeling that worry was just the beginning. For all of them.

'I, uh, I got some really choice magnesium samples.' Bobby spoke not because the magnesium samples were so very important, but because the silence was beginning to jangle his nerves. Jenny shot another sidelong glare at him, not taking her attention from the comms board, but knowing from experience what was coming next. No matter what he did, no matter who he had annoyed, irritated or hurt, Bobby stayed ashamed of Bobby for only so long. Then he went off on another tack and it was all forgotten – at least by him – until the next time. 'Where's Earl?'

Damn the boy! Can't he see what's happening …? Jenny MacLaine felt the wave of anger rising up through her like a hot tide, but crushed it back again with an effort. There would be time for that later. If they were lucky. Even so, she was unable to completely muffle the snap in her voice.

'Where d'ya think? With everybody else. Out battenin' down the perimeter.'

As Bobby blinked at her, still not fully understanding

the situation, she drew in a deep, calming breath that didn't calm her at all. If he didn't know by now, she'd just have to tell him straight. 'There was a skirmish out at the Northern Marker this morning.'

Even Bobby knew what that meant, and the realization hit him hard. Jenny saw the color drain out of his face, saw the way his mouth moved, shaping soundless explanations, excuses, maybe even apologies – for the first time in years. And all of them were too late, because nobody was listening any more. Nobody at all. From the sound of it, matters had gone beyond words this time. 'What?' he said at last. That was all he could manage.

'You know better than to go jackrabbiting around another Confederation's border.' At least, he should have known better. The subject had come up often enough. But oh no, not Bobby. 'Those hornets have been waiting for an excuse to take over this facility.'

Bobby blushed at the accusation, a quick surge of angry color coming into his pale face. 'I . . . I didn't know,' he said quickly. Too quickly. Jenny's mouth quirked downwards in silent disgust. It was just an excuse, like all the other times. An apology would have been just too much to hope for. 'I –'

Jenny pressed the ear-piece of the headset closer, and silenced him with a quick wave of her free hand. She had heard all Bobby's reasons before, and if she lived long enough, would probably hear them all again. But just now she was hearing something else; something that put a question-mark against long life for anyone down here.

'What? What is it?'

'It's those two that chased you,' Jenny said softly, trying to coax better reception from the outpost's elderly communication system. Earl had done his best with what they had, but Jenny knew well enough that what this radio needed wasn't so much regular maintenance as a few thousand extra dollars spent on upgrading it. Even so, lack of money or repair hadn't caused what she had just heard, and she needed to make sure that the words were real and accurate, instead of just a product of her scared imagination. Static whined and sizzled for a few seconds more. Then abruptly the signal cleared, a sure sign that it was being boosted through a commsat. Jenny flinched at what that might mean.

'They're on the satellite link,' she said quietly, 'calling their home base ...' *Register a formal complaint, damn you,* she thought at them. *Ask for advice. Legal enforcement. Sue us. Just don't do anything else. Don't ...*

The hornets didn't listen.

Oh God ...!

Jenny MacLaine felt a jolt in her chest as though her heart had stumbled against her ribs, and her eyes closed for an instant. It had been fine last checkup, but she knew that after a life with a lot of effort and little enough comfort in it, she was already at the age when a sudden shock might ... And then it went right on beating as if nothing had happened. She opened her eyes again, knowing now that things could get so bad that you're sure they can't get any worse. That was the stage when calm steps in.

'They're asking for military intervention.'

Bobby's eyes went wide, and he looked as though he was going to faint. Or throw up. Jenny watched him, feeling strangely detached from everything; from the young idiot who probably hadn't really started all this, because now it seemed as inevitable as winter after fall; from the frantic transmissions as everyone else along the Livingston Trench reacted to what she and they had heard; even from Earl, somewhere out there in the cold dark.

'What're we gonna do ...?' Fear and shock seemed to have driven Bobby's voice up an octave, so that he sounded more like the son she and Earl had always regarded him as and less like the thoughtless young roughneck he had become.

Jenny flipped switches on the console, opening her own channel up and out to another cold dark and the satellite hanging there waiting for her message, and summoned up the most reassuring smile she could manage.

'I guess,' she said as the system came on-line, 'say a prayer ...'

*

The initial response took almost eleven hours, and it was impossible to tell whose military backup was first to arrive on the scene; but they had not been first by more than a few minutes. Four submarines now waited above the disputed zone of the Livingston Trench, nose to nose in a rough circle only a few hundred meters across. It was a range more suited to fighting with knives than with torpedoes, but it was the accepted face-off procedure that had developed over a score of pointless encounters in every commercially-viable area of every ocean of the world. There were no visible markings on the black anechoic cladding of their hulls, and little enough difference in their outlines. Fifty years of sub design had seen to that. It was the same coincident evolution that had created similarities of shape for the dolphins, the killer whales and the great pelagic sharks. In design as in nature, form followed function – and the function here was to hunt and kill others of their own kind.

These warrior subs had many ancestors, vessels which in their time had been considered the best in the world: the *Alfa*, the *Victor* and the *Ak'yula* PLAs of the long-gone Soviet Union, and the Advanced-Albacore hullforms used by SSN attack boats in the old United States Navy and its allies. Some of those old boats had high, squared-off sails, others had lower and more streamlined fins like the cetacean shapes developed by the Russian subs, but all of their descendants were huge, rakish things. Menacingly sleek, sinister black shapes hanging deceptively placid in the water, steel sharks waiting for a feeding frenzy to begin.

And like a feeding frenzy, all it needed was blood in the water. A single wrong move would be enough for that. It wasn't enough that it hadn't happened yet. It only had to happen once.

*

Bobby leaned against the plastiform wall and watched the worried faces that filled the control-room. Not one of them had an expression that might have reassured him, and the only comfort was that not a one had looked at him with anything more than regret. At least there had been no blame. Not yet; and whether there would ever be depended very much on whether anyone survived to make the accusation that all this had been his fault. It probably wasn't. He was just the excuse, not the reason. *That* was reckoned in territory and in money value, the way it always had been.

The mining outpost was as crowded now as it ever got. Earl was back, and with him half a dozen other mine-workers with nowhere better to go. They were single men and women, gathered together here for some sort of comfort while the outside world decided their fate. Without, as usual, consulting them about it. That had been the fate of the little people all through history. Bobby shook his head. It was a bit late for philosophy; a course he had flunked anyway, in favor of auto-shop.

The most worried face in the entire room was one well away from ground zero: the EarthNet news anchor on the control-room TV monitor was doing a good job of whipping up the tension for all the other lucky people watching it from a safe distance. Though if this thing really blew, there might be no such thing as a safe distance anywhere on the planet ...

'... *Repeating once again – information has reached our Earthcast News studios in Greenwich that warrior submarines from several of the world's economic Confederations are converging on the Livingston Trench – a deep ocean canyon in the mid North Atlantic – and the threat of armed combat is suddenly dangerously real ...*'

The too-dramatic voice continued over a quick succession of military submarine schematics, world politico-economic graphics, and a slightly out-of-date Oceanographic Institute map of where all the action was. The monitor's video-vérité image shifted to a group of worried-looking people scrambling out of a shuttle on the helipad of the old United Nations Building in New York, and as Bobby looked at them, he thought callously that if they really wanted to know what worried was, they should be down here.

'... *Representatives from various Confederations are frantically meeting, trying to keep the situation from escalating, but ...'*

Bobby could see that Jenny was ignoring it. There was nothing she could do except continue to scan the radio bands for information, and considering how cluttered with information those bands were at the minute, she was doing so with consummate skill. Then she muttered something under her breath and her hands on the monitor board closed to fists. She straightened a little and looked up at Earl. Just Earl; not Bobby, nor anybody else. Right now for Jenny there probably *was* nobody else. 'The subs're all trying to reach their upworld bases,' she announced to the room in general, and though her voice was quiet it cut through the excited chatter from the monitor. 'They're trying to get the green light to open fire ...'

The other miners looked at each other, fear visible on weathered features that didn't know how to wear such a harsh emotion well. It was one thing to be scared by an equipment malfunction out in the mining fields, but at least that was something they knew how to handle. There wasn't a man or woman in the room who hadn't field-stripped unreliable digging gear and then put it back together, who didn't know what an out-of-place noise might mean and how to fix it. But this was different. Not all the expertise in the world could fix this situation, or make those subs go away – not without direct instructions from their surface command centers. It was the helplessness that was scary, even more than the threat.

'... Undersea territorial skirmishes have of course been occurring for years, but tensions seem to have reached the breaking point now at this very mineral-rich deep ocean trench. Observers have long pegged this region, where mining outposts from several different

Confederations coexist in dangerous proximity to one another, as a potential tinderbox ...'

None of which helped a damn. Bobby looked around him, at the faces of his friends, his workmates, at all the family he had, and not a one of them would meet his eye. Fear, like grief, was a private thing. He tried to filter out the ominous words of the broadcast, and for want of anything better to do, stared at the bank of external monitors. Passive sonar; magnetic anomaly detection; sound velocity; all of it was hardware that had been military secrets thirty years ago, and all that it could tell him was that nothing had changed. The four warrior subs were still out there in their standoff circle, not moving from their positions in case it might give one of the others a tactical advantage. The mining fields were dead; nothing was moving. Nobody would be so suicidal as to produce an echo-trace that might be mistaken for a hostile. Except ...

Bobby frowned. There was a trace on one of the scanners that *was* indicating movement, but in a location where no movement should be. Grateful for something to do to take his mind off useless fretting, he walked over to the readout and stared at it for a few seconds; then rapped the screen with his knuckle. The sharp sound made heads turn all over the control-room, and Bobby colored slightly at being the focus of attention. He waved vaguely at the scanner screen.

'Hey, uh, um, this reading is really screwy.'

It didn't deflect attention; rather the reverse, as a few other miners wandered over to see what was going on. A system glitch was something they knew how to deal with, which was more than could be said about the situation outside, and working on the notoriously quirky MacLaine system was at least better than standing helpless while the world's newspeople started some sort of countdown.

'It's the perimeter monitoring system,' said Bobby, rapping at it again. The trace jumped slightly, then steadied, and the digital scale of its echo-return began climbing for the first time. It shouldn't have been doing that. 'According to –' Bobby paused, looked again and shook his head. 'No, this can't be right. According to this, there's something down in the trench.'

That was impossible. The Livingston Trench wasn't as deep as some of the Pacific abyssals, but it was deep enough that any manned vessel apart from a bathyscaphe would only go into it one way. Down, right to the bottom, crushed flat as a dead beercan. Except that the source of this echo said otherwise. The scale readout began to tick over more quickly as the passive monitors picked up additional data; then it jumped to a blur of glowing numerals, slowed again, and held steady. Bobby stared, blinked, and for just an instant refused outright to believe what it was telling him.

'Something … *huge,*' he said at last, in an awestruck voice. 'And it's coming up …'

He saw Jenny turn to stare at him, and saw the doubt in her eyes. 'What kinda "something"?' Her voice was sharp, as skeptical as if she had caught him making excuses again. 'A ship?'

Bobby shook his head. He had no excuses this time, and no fake sincerity to get him off yet another hook. He didn't need them. The instruments said so. 'No ship I know gives off readings like this.' Then he looked from the instrument monitors to the low-light camera display, and his jaw dropped in disbelief. The news broadcast forgotten, everyone in the control-room crowded in to see.

It was something black, but glittering with lights; something moving, but so big that it seemed to stand still; something that none of them had ever seen out there before. Bobby took a step back from the monitors, and then another, as if scared the thing was going to come right through them, after him, once they gave it a shape.

'Wait a minute,' he said, and pointed at the bank of monitors as their computers enhanced the image and projected it on-screen. He *had* seen this thing before, bright with flags during its commissioning ceremony, but it was small wonder he hadn't recognised it. There were no flags now, just an aura of leashed-in power that he could almost feel. 'It was on the news. You remember . . .!' They stared at him for a few seconds as though he had taken leave of his senses, then someone laughed with pure relief.

Bobby stared at the great dark shape, the monster from the depths that had saved all their necks. He didn't laugh. All he could do was smile . . . But now, he felt like it. Because he knew the monster's name.

'*seaQuest*!'

TWO

A somber leviathan rose out of the Livingston Trench.

On this vessel there was no dorsal sail, no cylindrical hull, no control empennage. Instead the sleek, flattened bow and the sweeping curves of the main body looked . . . not so much unfamiliar as unearthly, an alien shape that had hair-raising echoes of the giant squid. And not just any squid, but an abyssal kraken, the whale-killing nightmare of the deep dark. In a slow, arrogant display of size and power, it glided effortlessly upward into the center of the face-off circle and hovered there, dwarfing the four warrior submarines, defying them to challenge, confident they would not dare.

This was *seaQuest*. It had been designed to fulfil a single function: to be the best. The most efficient, the fastest and the deadliest military submarine on Earth. There was a certain grim curiosity, both among those who had designed and built it and those who now crewed it into yet another state of near-but-never war, about how good that design was; about what it could really do. But until someone gave the proper orders, there was no way to find out . . .

*

The atmosphere on *seaQuest*'s Bridge jangled with tension. This situation, and all the others like it, had been going on for fifteen years, ever since the first attempt to register a territorial claim to areas of the ocean floor had been backed up by force. Some of the crew had been involved since the beginning, others were young enough that all their experience had been aboard this boat.

It made very little difference either way. She had been at sea for almost two years, a vessel designed to be so much better than all the rest that some sort of an end might be put to this endless bickering. And in those two years, no-one in the North Pacific Confederation had dared pass on the command to fire. A century and a half ago, the hand-cranked CSS *Hunley* had been more dangerous than *seaQuest* was now, because that crew had at least been granted clearance to do something with their weapons. And the superiors who had authorized that clearance had been able to transmit their message ...

'Captain! Nor-Pac Command is trying to get through! But it's breaking up. There's heavy Sat-Link interference!'

Captain Marilyn Stark glanced at the communications station, but said nothing at first. She spent a few more seconds studying Chief Maxwell's sensor displays before bothering to answer, then said, 'Keep trying, Lieutenant.'

That was all. Confidence in her crew had been Stark's trademark all through her career. She had spent half her life in the service, both on and under the surface, and it took more than a cranky radio to crack her glacial calm. Communications Officer Mack O'Neill had learned his trade on comms boards that had been the cutting edge of military technology, and they had been archaic by comparison with the equipment aboard *seaQuest*. Stark knew that even if it wasn't working properly, it would be telling him why not: and that way a good Comms Officer could start doing something about it.

She was aware that *seaQuest* was right at the limit for Nor-Pac's geostationary relay satellite, and that was where most of the problem lay. Its boosted laser-optical transmission was barely able to penetrate the deep layer of water between submarine and surface, and what signal managed to leak through was being degraded both by depth and by the active jamming of the other four warrior subs. But there were ways around that. As she looked at him again, O'Neill was already feeding in the sequence that would deploy *seaQuest*'s half-kilometer ELF antenna; at seven minutes for a three-letter code group, the Extremely-Low-Frequency unit's data transfer rate was incredibly slow, but it was reliable – and almost impossible to jam. Stark turned back to Maxwell.

'Deploy Whiskers,' she told the sensor chief, with no more change in her voice than if she had ordered a cup of coffee, and reached out to indicate points on the main WSKR screen. 'Narrow cone sweeps.' She straightened and pressed both hands into the small of her back, easing away a kink and stretching her spine like a lazy cat waiting for a mouse. Then she tapped a secondary board on the sensor console. 'Feed all data directly to fire control.'

That was unexpected, and not one of the accepted moves in the game. Maxwell looked at her, and she saw him lick his lips nervously before risking a reply. 'Aye-aye, Captain.' He worked over his console. 'Whiskers out – feeding data now.'

The sound of the acknowledgement was shaky. Stark gave him a hard smile and a reassuring pat on the shoulder, made a mental note to keep an eye on him, then turned toward her command chair.

'Four plasma torpedoes charged and loaded,' sang out Phillips, the Weapons Officer. Stark favoured him with a quick approving glance, because he spoke in a briskly efficient tone that Stark recognized as an unconscious echo of her own. At another time, in another place, she might have been amused. Now it simply reassured her that he would carry out her orders without question. At this time, in this place, any hesitation could kill them all.

'Thank you, Mr Phillips.' She didn't ask for any other information; on any vessel under Marilyn Stark's command, there was never any need for the Captain to waste breath. If her crew had something to say, they said it – otherwise they got back to their duties.

Halfway to the chair she met her Executive Officer, and automatically looked him over for traces of the same strain she had detected in Maxwell. She could see none. Though Jonathan Ford was as weary as everyone else on the seaQuest's Bridge, and hadn't bothered to hide the fact, he was managing to keep all other concerns and emotions bottled up inside. That control was one of the reasons why he had made the rank of Lieutenant Commander so fast, and his present position as the youngest Exec in the fleet. Not bad for a poor black kid from East Chicago, an escapee from the dreadful and violent life of the gangs. Her own reports had been partially responsible for his swift ascent through the ranks – Captain Stark did not hand out such commendations lightly – but the rest of it had been thanks to Ford's own abilities. Without them there would have been no commendations anyway.

The Exec looked quickly towards O'Neill at the comms

station, but got only a shake of the head. 'Still no clear message from Nor-Pac Command,' he said. 'I guess the other subs are also calling for orders.'

Stark knew that much already. At least with *seaQuest*'s state-of-the-art communications gear, if any instructions were trying to filter through the natural and man-made interference, hers would get here first. The knowledge didn't make her any happier. 'Dammit!' she snapped. 'How many of these standoffs are we going to have before somebody makes a decision?'

'I figure as long as none of those other captains lose their cool, nothing ugly's gonna happen,' said Ford with a reassurance none of them really felt. Cool or not, there was always the X-factor; errors, accidents, malfunctions. Too many risks.

Captain Stark nodded distantly. *Like all the other times.* 'And we'll all move away,' she said. 'Continue our patrols. Always waiting. Always on the brink.'

Like someone who climbs to the high board, she thought ... but never takes the dive. Do that enough times and people will start to believe you don't have the nerve, and never will. They won't show you any respect. They'll think you're a coward, an easy mark, a pushover – because when it comes to the hard shove, you've always backed down before, and why should this time be any different? And when that finally happens, a lot of people are going to get killed. Better to lose a few right now, and get back the respect.

'How many of these stalemates have we engaged in over the past twenty months ...?' she muttered to herself. Ford heard her plainly enough, but said nothing; the question hadn't been directed at him, and most likely didn't need an answer in any case. Dropping into the command chair, Stark looked around the Bridge. Everyone was at their post, intent on doing an efficient job, even though when the orders finally came through that job would likely be to disengage from combat stance and return to another standard patrol routine.

Until the next time. Or the time after that. Stark grimaced inwardly. This was a good crew, maybe the best she had ever commanded, and the constant roundabout of alerts and stand-downs was running them ragged, blunting their edge. It was *wasting* them. She gestured past the Exec, a quick sweep of the hand that took in not just the Bridge but the entire boat, and all the skills, all the weapons, all the potential that it contained. Reluctantly, Stark let just a little of the anger inside her creep into the open.

'Don't they understand that the only way to secure the peace is by strength? That this cat-and-mouse game will go on forever unless somebody makes a stand?' She looked sidelong at Ford. 'This crew is *ready*. We've been ready for years.' He said nothing, and that was as Stark expected. Ford, and all the command cadre aboard *seaQuest*, knew how capable the personnel aboard this boat could be if Nor-Pac Command just gave them the chance. But they didn't know, *couldn't* know, how deeply the Captain felt about it.

'My father faced a similar situation in Vietnam,' she said. 'Nineteen sixty-nine. Just a few years before I was born. Enemy right in his sights, superior firepower and tactical advantage. But he couldn't get through to his command for the green light.' She glanced hopefully at communications, only to get another head-shake from O'Neill. 'You know what he thought of? Something my grandfather the General told him. Sometimes there's nobody to give you orders. Sometimes you gotta weigh up a situation and make your own choice. Just so long as you're ready to stand by it, right or wrong.'

She saw Ford's expression change; just a little, but enough that his face couldn't hide what he was thinking any more. The story – and the connotations behind it – had unsettled him, and it showed. His problem: if he wanted to make any higher than Exec, if he wanted a command of his own, it was time he started considering all the implications of command decisions. The bad as well as the good ones.

'My father weighed the situation, he made the choice, he stood by it. And he took the shot. It earned him his gold bars.' Stark finished speaking in a soft voice that was more for herself than for Ford. Then she rotated the Command chair towards the helm station. 'Come around, two-zero-niner and hold her steady.'

'But we're not at war, Captain,' she heard Ford say behind her.

Marilyn Stark's lips thinned in a tight, humorless smile as she mentally scrawled *unsuited to promotion beyond present rank* across her Executive Officer's file. 'Neither was he. Officially.'

The deck tilted slightly as *seaQuest*'s bow began to swing, then evened up as the helmsman stabilized his controls. 'One-niner-five, two-zero-zero, two-zero-five, zero-seven ... Holding at two-zero-niner, Captain, and steady as she goes.'

At the main sensor suite, Maxwell started punching buttons. 'Whisker data coming in! Four class C shooter subs ...'

The big main screens had been showing computer-enhanced views of the four threat subs since *seaQuest* came up out of the trench. They had been nothing but plain-vanilla observation images – until now. The new displays of relative bearing and range-to-target data scrolling along the sides of the screen were meant for much more than just observation.

'Target status?' Stark rapped at Maxwell. She could sense Ford moving closer behind her, and feel the pressure as his fingers dug into the padding of the chair.

'Captain, may I remind you that –'

'Not now, Commander.' The hard, flat voice was almost a dismissal, and Stark ignored him. Ford might be on her Bridge, but so far as she was concerned, right now he was no longer a useful part of her crew. 'Mister Maxwell ...?'

The sensor chief eyed his monitors like a man staring down the barrel of a gun. 'All targets – seventy-eight percent vulnerability. We're locked in attack position.'

'Target grids.'

'Grids activated.'

The system was already on standby; it powered up at once, throwing targeting pinpoints over the primary strike areas on each enemy vessel. Stark favored the four submarines on the forward screens with a speculative stare, then opened the covered panel set into the arm of her chair and flipped an independent-use weapons control panel up out of its recess.

The Bridge went very quiet, and Stark saw several crewmen exchange worried glances. She could understand why, and even sympathize with them. This was getting too close. *seaQuest* had never gone weapons-free in any of the past encounters with other Confederation vessels. Now she had done so without orders, on nothing but her own captain's discretion.

But that big step had to be taken some day, and who better to take it than somebody at the sharp end, somebody who had more immediate concerns than votes and public opinion. Somebody who had the training to see an opportunity and put it to good use. Somebody like Marilyn Stark ...

seaQuest's torps were loaded, the tubes flooded, the bow-caps open to the sea, and with the Whiskers deployed there was no need even for the betraying ping of a targeting sonar. Just like her father: *enemy right in his sights, superior firepower and tactical advantage.* The parallels were too close for this to be a mistake.

'Captain. I *strongly* recommend that we wait for clear orders from Nor-Pac ...' Ford leaned over the Command chair, his voice pitched low, doing her the courtesy of keeping their difference of opinion private. For the time being.

Stark returned that courtesy by deigning to notice his existence again. She gazed up at him from the chair, noting the sweat on his skin, the fright in his eyes, the reluctance to admit that she was right. No, she concluded; not suited to command rank at all.

'Clear orders? Aren't you tired of this game?' she said, jerking her chin towards the main screens and the target displays that glowed on them. It looked like a computer game indeed, though for a higher score than mere points. 'We aim at them, they aim at us, and the world waits. For what? Nothing. Until the next time. Everybody's too afraid to fire. Afraid of what it might start. They're forgetting that if you want to finish something, you have to start it first.'

She slapped her hand against the chair, close enough to the control board's firing toggle that she saw him wince. 'We *shouldn't* be afraid. Look at this boat: the "ultimate war ship". We have the strength and the advantage. Don't you understand? We have an opportunity to end this madness once and for all. Do what we've been trained to do.'

Her voice rose, so that heads turned all over the Bridge. She didn't care any more; this matter had gone beyond mere theoretical discussion. It was only right that the crew of the finest submarine in the fleet should know what the best captain in the fleet intended for them. Glory ...

'I've weighed up the situation for years, Mr Ford,' she said, and grinned at him. 'I've known this decision would have to be made sooner or later. But I'll stand by it. My name deserves a place in the history books. Maybe they'll mention you, too. ....'

O'Neill's urgent voice cut through anything else Stark might have said. The Comms Officer was almost on his feet with excitement and relief. 'Captain!' It was just short of a shout. 'Confirmed orders are coming in from Nor-Pac Command: Do Not Fire! Repeat: *Do Not Fire!*' He recovered control of himself as the entire Bridge crew let out a collective sigh of relief, and delivered the rest of the message in a more normal voice. 'The other subs are receiving similar orders ...'

The Captain didn't move. Stark gazed fixedly at the main screens as if she hadn't heard – or had decided not to listen. They wanted her to back down again. To deny her ancestry, to throw away the accumulated respect of generations just because they were afraid of the consequence of actions they were afraid to take. Nothing but fear and lack of resolution. *Lack of moral fibre.* In older times, soldiers had been discharged from the service for that; or put up against a wall and shot. Somebody had to take a stand. Somebody like Marilyn Stark ...

Her hand moved towards the firing-toggle.

'Captain ...!'

The cold stare she shot at Ford was no different than the way she had been gazing at the target submarines. It held a promise of imminent disciplinary measures, on top of a demand that he be transferred somewhere, anywhere, just so long as it was off *seaQuest*. A man like that didn't deserve to stand on the Bridge of a boat like this, to be part of a crew like this, to serve under a captain like this.

'History is waiting, Lieutenant. And *I* won't make the excuse that I was only following orders ...'

She reached for the toggle, but Ford's hand was there first, slapping it back down into its molded recess to disarm the weapons control. Then he grasped her arm and held it, preventing her from reactivating the system. Stark glared at the fingers on her wrist, unable to believe the evidence of her own eyes. It had gone beyond the countermanding of an order: this was *mutiny!*

'I can't let you do it, Captain.' Ford sounded anguished, whether from the fear she had seen so plainly on his face, or because he still respected her and hated what he was doing. Good, bad or indifferent, the reasons didn't matter to Stark. Only the action they had prompted. Her eyes narrowed, a focus for the fury burning behind them.

'You are relieved, Mister!' The voice was a whipcrack, a sound that in all her fleet career had never been disobeyed. If Ford wouldn't back down, Maxwell or one of the others would come up here and make him. It had always been that way before; there was no reason why it shouldn't be that way again.

She was wrong ...

THREE

Thirteen months later the darkness had passed and there was light everywhere.

The burning blueness of clear afternoon light in the Caribbean is hard to believe even when you're in the middle of it. Sky mirrors sea, and sea reflects sky ... until the eye is baffled and looks for somewhere to rest, anywhere, any difference of color. It soon finds that difference, for here in particular the sea is not just one color. The warmth and clarity of the water clearly reveal what more northerly seas cannot – detail of color and texture on the bottom, and most particularly, detail of depth. Here and there, offshore, as the whites and pinks of sand shade down through pale aqua toward turquoise and cyan, there appears something abrupt to break the smooth transition of shades – a sudden patch or hole of pure deep indigo, indicator of much deeper water, a blue hole leading downwards and perhaps away. The seabottoms are not solid here: they have known too much activity in the past four or five millennia, and caves and substrate tunnels are everywhere in the warm darkness, for those who know how to find them.

One of those who did was gliding some feet under the surface, over the deep downward plunge of one of those holes, when he heard the noise overhead. The dolphin cocked his head upward; even with the poor conductivity that comes with airborne sound impacting into water, he could tell it was nothing normal. He headed topside.

As his sleek, beaked head broke surface, the noise became almost unbearable, ratcheting and howling against his skin, a deep, thrumming roar that slapped across the water of the lagoon and drove outraged birds skyward from every tree in sight. He winced a bit and looked up as the blocky, angular shape whooshed across the water. It was riding across the waves in a churn of creamy foam, moving as fast as a shark, but nowhere near as quietly. It headed for the shores of the island which surrounded this hole in the water, slowed as it surged up onto the beach, then began to settle downward, kicking up a great storm of sand and noise as it did so. Finally it was still on the sand, and the dolphin looked at it for a moment as something like a mouth began to open in its side. He could see movement in the shadows within. That made up his mind about what to do, and with much less fuss than the hovercraft had produced, he dived again.

*

From a blue pool not too far away, the dolphin's shape broke surface; and then, right by it, a man stood up from the water, wearing a suntan and nothing else. He shook the water out of his hair and made his way to the shore with the fish he had speared, shook out the clothes which had been hanging on a nearby branch, slipped into them, and started into the undergrowth.

The man walked up the path he had made through the tropical plants, brushing them aside, occasionally muttering as one of them sprang back and hit him in the eye. *I should take a machete to these things, they're getting out of hand again*, he thought, *but who has time?* He switched the spear and fish to the other hand, shrugged to resettle the monitoring device slung over his shoulder on its worn strap, pushed back another big branch of bougainvillea, and stepped out into the fringes of the clearing –

– and stopped. There were people, uniformed people, outside his house. Practically *inside* it.

The eyes in his craggy face tightened like a trap about to snap shut. He could just imagine what they thought of the house. Well, the outside of it, anyway, just a thatched shack on stilts: but the way they were foregathered on the ramp leading up to his front door, goggling at the inside, suggested that the house's contents had caught them by surprise. *Good*, he thought, annoyed.

He paused a moment, considering, and then decided to take it lightly. He came out from under the shelter of the palms and strode up among them, whistling, finally shouldering them aside – politely enough – as he went up the ramp. 'Excuse me. Pardon me. Stepping past ... so sorry ...'

Right past their astonished faces he went, and into the house, feeling them staring at him from behind, and smiling slightly at their discomfiture. If they had been surprised by what was in the house, heaven only knew what they thought of him: tanned dark, scruffy-bearded, carrying a wickedly sharp fishing spear with three big bluefish impaled on it, wearing an ancient faded Hawaiian shirt and old khaki shorts, sandals, and the baseball cap he had woven himself out of palm fronds, with the scribbled intertwined NY of the Yankees on it. *A sight*, he said, glancing around to make sure that no one had slipped in and touched his equipment.

There was enough of it, but it was mostly the kitchen side of it he was interested in at the moment. He had cleaned the bluefish down by the water: now he slipped them off the spear, picked up a knife, and started to work on them. The visitors took the excuse to slide into the main room behind him, staring at everything. Well might they stare. Packed into this twelve-by-twelve space, racked up against the rough walls, was enough scientific equipment to remind a casual observer of a homemade Mission Control, or possibly some old TV starship's bridge. All carefully chosen over a matter of years to do exactly what he needed, regardless of price: the banked instruments and their controlling computers sat quietly doing their jobs on storage power.

One of the people, a woman, stepped forward and looked at him. She was uniformed like the rest, tropical shirt-sleeve order, with the rank-bars of a full commander on her shoulderboards and a dinky little badge that said 'Webber' over one shirt pocket. 'Captain Bridger ...?'

He shook his head, put the first bluefish aside, started in on the second. 'Bridger?' he said, flattening the fish with a crunch to get backbone and ribs all out in one. 'Bridger ... Not around here. Have you tried the other side of the island, around 77th Street? I think there's a Bridger over that way. Mind you, he leaves for work early, so you better hurry . . .' He inclined his head to her, the gesture of two strangers meeting in the street, and eased past; then looked at another of the intruders and gave this man a long, slow top-to-toe examination. 'Nice outfit.' That was all.

Webber looked at him incredulously, then beckoned to the officer whose neat recruiting-office appearance had been so casually dismissed. He stepped up beside her and offered a readout on a small pad. Webber glanced at it, then nodded and smiled.

The second fish was done: the scruffy beachcomber reached sideways for a pan, poured a little olive oil into it, ignoring the two who looked from the readout to him again. 'The man we're looking for is *Nathan* Bridger,' persisted Webber. 'Former American Naval Captain – served nine years in the North Pacific Confederation forces. Submarine commander. Everybody, including his enemies – *especially* his enemies – called him the best.'

How touching. He reached for a peppermill. 'Can't help ya, darlin'. Don't know the guy. Sorry. I'm just a hungry scientist.' He gave her a cheerfully roguish wink that put her momentarily off-balance, so that she had to consult the readout again.

'Marine geology,' she read, not bothering to conceal the increasingly dubious edge in her voice. 'Advanced degree. Decorated seven times . . .'

'Eight,' he said absently, then glanced at his watch. 'O'clock. Boy, where does the day go?' He shrugged his shoulders and paid no attention at all to the satisfied smile crossing Commander Webber's face. That little slip had been enough for her, but there were more important matters to hand. Breakfast, for one. He put the pan over the little gas burner, swirling it to be sure the oil heated evenly. Scorched bluefish was dreadful: not even the *aioli* sauce would save it. The oil popped and spat, and he frowned. Too hot. He reached for the control knob on the burner and lowered the flame, totally engrossed in cooking and very obviously not in the least interested by anyone or anything else.

Webber cleared her throat and Nathan raised one eyebrow. This was obviously the Important Part. 'Sir,' she said, 'we've come here at the request of UEO Command ...'

'Who?' Nathan looked at another of the bluefish, this one intact, and then at Webber. He dropped the fish onto the chopping-block and studied it thoughtfully, then stared at Webber some more. She glanced at the fish, colored slightly, then cleared her throat again.

'The United Earth/Oceans Organization,' she explained, and by now there was a little more long-suffering patience in her voice than was really necessary.

'Doesn't ring a bell,' said Nathan. He picked up a machete that was definitely not a kitchen knife. 'But then, I'm a little out of touch.'

Still staring at Webber, he brought the machete down with a quick, hard thump that lopped the bluefish's head clean off. It went tumbling from his kitchen counter almost on top of the Commander's immaculately shiny shoes, and she stared down at it for several awkward seconds. The fish stared back, and if Bridger thought there was any other similarity between it and Commander Webber, he was too much of a gentleman to say so out loud.

'Captain, we've gone to great lengths to find you,' she started again.

Nathan looked her in the eye, and his forced good

humor began to evaporate. Maybe that message hadn't been obvious enough for a thick-skinned career swabbo after all. 'Well, I hate to burst your bubble,' he said coldly, 'but you've wasted your time.' He turned his back on her and stalked towards the door.

'Captain ...'

Doesn't she ever take no for an answer? Enough is enough! Nathan felt the suppressed anger flare up inside him as he swung around on her. 'Hey, I don't know what you people are selling – but I'm not interested!' He took a step forward until he and Commander Webber were almost nose to nose. 'Now do me a favor – *and get the hell off my island ...!'*

It was the sound of the old Nathan Bridger, eight times decorated, full Captain, as much in command on the floor of this shack as on the bridge of a warship. Webber's brows drew together and her mouth opened; then wisely she shut it again and took a step backward. It gave him enough room to slip past her and head out of there, fast, right out to the ramp –

– and to stop at the sight of yet another man standing at the ramp's bottom, looking up at him. Another one in uniform. But the face –

'Hello, Nathan,' he said.

Bill. William Noyce. *Admiral* William Noyce. He was grinning. Not Webber's smile, that had so set his teeth on edge, but the grin of a man genuinely pleased to see an old friend again. *Oh, what the hell are you doing here ...?* As if he really needed to wonder.

'I should have known you were behind this.'

'Nice to see you again too. It's been some time, buddy. Six years!' Bill stepped forward, the grin getting bigger, oblivious to everything but the happy reunion –

No way, Nathan thought. He headed down the ramp, letting his face harden over. 'Go home, Bill,' he said. 'Uh-uh. I'm not doing this. I told you, I never wanted to talk to you, to *anyone*, from those days, ever again. So just –' Several possibilities suggested themselves, but this was Bill Noyce and a friend, not that hardnose Webber. He was already being quite rude enough. 'Just go home.'

He pushed past Noyce, heading toward the path through the jungle. 'Nathan, listen!' Bill shouted after him. 'Things have changed! Will you just listen? The *world* has changed! Dammit, let me explain!'

He tried to shut the voice out, to lose it as he plunged back into the sheltering greenness. It didn't work. 'Nathan, she's finished!' Bill shouted. 'She's been operational for three years!'

For just that moment Nathan stopped. Swallowed. Then he went on into the jungle again, desperate to leave the past behind him ...

... and afraid that it might already be too late: afraid that, after all this while, he was once again snared and struggling in the present ...

*

He had set up a workspace by the blue hole where he and the dolphin had been working: not much more than a rough-hewn table with a tin canopy over it, enough to protect the generator and the various old weathered bench-pull equipment from the sudden squalls that often came up here. The most valuable piece of equipment, though, was one that he wasn't worried about getting wet. Now Nathan knelt by the edge of the blue hole, strapping it to the dolphin. It was a handmade harness, the strap on one side pocketed to take the electronic sensor pack which relayed depth and temperature information to the racked equipment waiting above.

Nathan was making sure of the last few fastenings when he heard the footsteps coming into the clearing behind him. He ignored their source, for the moment, though he saw the interested look the dolphin threw them.

Nathan stood up. 'Okay, Darwin. You know the routine.' He made the hand motions which were the only part of the communication he was sure the dolphin understood. 'Tag the machine. Three levels down. Understand? Three.'

Darwin just floated there, turned sideways a little, one of those dark eyes looking up at him. One flipper slapped at the water, splashing him.

Nathan breathed out. 'Darwin – dammit. Don't get cute. I'm not in the mood.' He bent down with the beacon and put its strap into the toothy mouth with its fixed smile, then repeated the handsignals. 'Three levels down.'

Darwin floated a moment more, that eye regarding Nathan: then flipped his tail, rolled upside down and dove down into the blue water. Not for the first time, Nathan stood there wondering, *What goes on inside that head? How much does he understand of what's going on?* There was, of course, no hope of answers. But the companionship of even so different a creature was reward enough; answers weren't everything.

Just *almost* everything ...

He moved to the table and had a look at the instruments, checking the bathymeter. Thirty meters down already: Darwin was going about his business with dispatch.

'Hand-motion communication?' Noyce's voice said from

behind him. 'Including numericals. With a specimen born in the wild. Pretty impressive.'

Nathan opened his mouth to let out one of several possible retorts, then scrapped it, and instead said, 'It's not perfect, but we understand each other. Which is more than I can say for you and me.'

Noyce didn't respond to the jab. Instead he came to stand beside Nathan, peering at the equipment, nodding a little. 'As I remember, it was Carol who got you interested in dolphins,' Noyce said into the silence, for there was something a little odd about it. 'I heard about what happened. I'm sorry. She was a wonderful woman.'

The bathymeter was ticking away to itself, set on 'record' as always: it hardly needed his attention. Nathan glanced sideways at Noyce, suddenly suspicious. 'How'd you know?'

'C'mon, Nathan. You don't think the Navy is about to let one of its most valuable human resources run off to some island like this and not keep tabs on him?' Nathan grimaced: Noyce ignored it. 'You're not *entirely* isolated here. You trade the data you collect with passing research ships in return for supplies and equipment.'

'And when they leave, you shake them down for information about me. Great. Whatever happened to an individual's right to privacy? – The United States may be part of the North Pacific Confederation now, but last I heard the Bill of Rights was still alive and well ...'

The anger in his voice should have warned Noyce off. But he didn't move: and to Nathan's surprise, his voice held more compassion in it than anything else. 'I also know that with Carol gone, your one passion is your research. And in the last year your work has reached an impasse.

You've learned all you can from this rock. And you're frustrated as hell.'

Nathan turned his attention back to the machinery, which didn't need it: moved a gain control, made a couple of other unnecessary adjustments. 'Everything's *changed*, Nathan,' Noyce said. His voice was almost pleading. 'There's been a truce. We're *trying*. I've come halfway around the world to tell you about it.'

Nathan turned away, not wanting to deal with the hope and fear in Bill's voice, not wanting to deal with *any* of it: old memories, old imperatives, suddenly reasserting themselves. Beside him, Noyce signalled to one of Webber's team. It was the young fashion-plate officer again; he hurried forward, saluted, handed Noyce something, then retreated.

'You remember in the academy, we'd pull those all-nighters?' Noyce said, sounding reflective. 'A couple of times a week, at least. ...'

There was certainly no forgetting *that*. 'Trying to absorb all the ideas and theories old man Danielson would throw at us,' Nathan said. It had been dreadful, wringing work, all of them constantly ridden by the fear of failure, of looking bad to Danielson, or worse, to each other – proud young pups that they had been.

'What was the one thing that got us through those nights?' Bill said.

Involuntarily, Nathan's mouth began to water. 'That red licorice ice cream from the cadet lounge ...'

Something cold nudged him in the arm. Surprised, Nathan turned, looked down – at a metallic gallon carton, the contents cream striped with red – and two spoons.

'Nathan,' Bill said. 'All I want to do is talk ...'

*

They left Webber's team behind and walked off down the beach together, each man passing the carton to the other as his hands got too cold to keep holding it. Nathan devoted himself to enjoying the ice cream, and otherwise tried desperately not to show how all this intrigued him, how the news from his old world made him bizarrely eager for more ...

'Once the UN collapsed in twenty-eleven, the whole thing started to unravel,' Bill was saying. 'Well, you know. Undersea borders went up, nations split into Confederations to protect their territorial claims. The world lived under the constant threat of war. ... That's the world you turned your back on. And that *was* our world ... Then thirteen months ago, everything changed.'

'Livingston Trench.'

Noyce's eyebrows shot up in surprise, and Nathan could see the quick tumble of questions go through his mind. Questions like *how?*, like *when?*, like *what else does this bearded beachcomber know that he's not telling?* 'You know about it?'

Bridger shrugged elaborately and stared out at the lagoon. 'Bits and pieces,' he said dismissively. He didn't offer any other answers about where he'd acquired the information, and Noyce was good enough not to pressure him. The Admiral had already guessed he wasn't as isolated – or as disinterested – as he was pretending. *So what. That didn't change anything.*

'Shooter subs from different Confederations faced each other down,' said Noyce quietly. He looked at Nathan,

44

then held up his right hand, finger and thumb almost touching. 'We came *this* close to blowing up the whole damn planet. It really looked like it was going to happen. But – it didn't. Thank God. But we came so close ...' There was an expression in Bill Noyce's dark eyes that told Nathan all he needed to know; all, and much more.

'So close that the Confederation governments started to talk. They hammered out a peace agreement. The United Earth/Oceans Organization was formed to administer it.'

Nathan smiled slightly: he knew a sales pitch when he heard one. 'Administer ... Sounds desperate. And it's been working for a whole year now. Wow.'

'It's been working ... and I'm a part of it. Part of the UEO.'

Nathan stared at him, astonished. *A career-Navy type like Bill ...?* 'You left Nor-Pac Command?'

Noyce nodded. 'Because I think this could be the real thing this time, Nathan.' He looked out at the ocean. 'It's quite a bit different out there from when you last saw it. Not just scientific installations and mining facilities. There are farms, and colonies. *Families.* But it's very much a frontier, and there are still a lot of ... problems. People from the old days got used to taking what they wanted. Sometimes they still do. So UEO needed a way to maintain the situation.' He walked on a little, then stopped and looked back at Nathan. 'That's why Nor-Pac gave us the *seaQuest* ...'

Nathan blinked. He thought he had been surprised before, but it was nothing to *this*. How many billions of research and development dollars, how much for the actual building – and they *gave* her away –? It was unthinkable; not just because of the money involved, but because of

45

the power. All that, in independent hands ... He remembered what *seaQuest*'s weapons systems had looked like on the drawing-board, and despite the heat baking off the sand, Nathan shivered.

'Not as a warship,' said Noyce. 'As a peacekeeper.'

'There's a difference?'

'What vessel is better suited? And –' he looked significantly at Nathan – 'she's being refitted to include a large science contingent on board.'

'What do you mean, "large science contingent"? And what for?'

'Research, Nathan. Deep ocean research. The largest deep submergence research vessel *ever*. Think about it.'

Nathan thought. After a moment he said, 'Why are you here, Bill?'

Noyce just looked at him. His silence confirmed everything.

'*Oh*, no,' Nathan said. 'No way! That – that part of my life is over. It doesn't ... It doesn't exist any more.' He turned away from the sea and began to walk back up the beach.

Noyce stared at his receding back, and his patience ran out. 'Don't you understand what I'm offering you?' he shouted in frustration. 'Nathan, you can't pass this up!' Bridger kept on walking. It was very obvious that he could, and would, and to all intents and purposes already had. 'For God's sake, Carol's dead! Let it go.'

Nathan stopped. 'No,' he said at last. 'I can't.'

'Why not?'

Nathan turned. For a long, silent time he stared at his old friend, knowing full well that it was only their friendship which had stopped him from retracing his steps and

46

planting his fist in Bill Noyce's face for what he had just said. His mouth worked under the scruffy beard, shaping and discarding all the things he needed to say so that what he wanted to do would make some sort of sense. None of them worked. 'Because,' he began at last, and then his voice and his temper flared together. 'Because I gave her my word!'

He stood there, breathing hard, his fists clenched. Captains did not give a bawling-out to Admirals, and even a close friendship could be put in jeopardy by the spleen and bitterness he had just dumped on Bill Noyce's head. Nathan watched and waited for the reaction; but Bill just shook his head. This was nothing. What was done was done, and an outburst of simple pain was far from the worst.

'I know how much losing Eric hurt you,' he said softly. 'How you blame yourself for him joining the service. I have kids too, remember ...?' He made a small gesture that took in the lagoon, the beach, the trees; all of them empty, a beautiful desolation without a trace of humanity except for the small uniformed figures in the distance, and the two of them. 'But Nathan, look around you. You're totally alone here. Don't you see how your research – your *passion* – could be served aboard a boat *you* poured your life and heart and soul into?' He looked at Nathan, and there was nothing sly or conniving in his expression. 'Just come *see* her. Step aboard. Let me show you what I'm talking about. Carol wouldn't mind that, would she?'

Even before he opened his mouth to reply, someone had guessed what that answer might be. Nathan could already hear the growing thunder of the hovercraft's engines. He looked at Bill, then looked at the sea, and he thought. The thoughts went round and around, and led nowhere ...

*

Some hours later, changed into worn chinos and a different shirt, Nathan knelt by the edge of the blue hole; the dolphin, out of his harness now, floated there and watched him.

'Darwin,' Nathan said quietly, 'it won't be long. I'll be back real soon.' He made the hand-signs for *return*, *soon*, and one he had never been sure how wholly the dolphin had grasped: *not worry*. Nathan was vaguely aware of Noyce, behind him, fiddling with his portable communicator; he ignored it. Noyce understood what was happening. How much Darwin understood was hard to say, so reassurance was more important than hurrying anywhere else.

And reassurance was definitely what was needed. The symbologies of island and womb, of retreat, avoidance, denial, were not lost on Nathan. He had rejected them for a long time. Now, though ... having to leave, even when it was his own curiosity that drove him ... it was a wrench.

The dolphin chittered softly: a sound that had often been a reply to the 'don't worry' sign. Nathan stroked that incredibly soft skin one more time, and very gently tapped the bulging forehead, the 'melon' or sonar-sensing organ, twice quickly: *see you soon*.

Darwin looked at him obliquely out of that bright eye, then turned and dove away, showing him, sidewise, the eternal smile.

Nathan's heart clenched with fear: for whom, it was uncertain. He got up, picked up his small bag of belongings, and followed Bill Noyce to the waiting hovercraft. The business of shutting doors, the engine revving, almost passed him by: as soon as he sat down, Nathan's whole attention went to the view outside the window, always open before, now encapsulated in glass and steel, unreal, remote. The craft lifted away from the beach in a storm of sand, and the view outside that window contracted from a blaze of green and white to a spot of green in a wider glare of blue; a green eye, a blue pupil, looking back at him, dropping away behind him, lost.

He took in a long, slow, deliberate breath of the foreign air inside the hovercraft – it was cool, metal-smelling, conditioned and thoroughly man-made, and totally unlike the air he had been breathing on the island – and turned away from the window to see the new world Bill had promised him.

FOUR

At first, Nathan had been slightly at a loss. He walked around *seaQuest* feeling rather like a six-year-old on his first day in kindergarten: abruptly deserted among others, almost all strangers, who looked at him with expressions of uncertainty and unease. *That may be* the *Nathan Bridger*, they seemed to be thinking, *but he still looks like a goddamn beachcomber* ...

But he would not let them see his unease for any money – not even Crocker's genuine antique greenbacks – or guess at it either: so finally he went wandering again. He walked from one end of *seaQuest* to the other, on all her levels, poking his head into labs, peering at staterooms, putting his nose into the engine room, the computer-support and prep rooms, even the galley (which despite its shining newness was like every other sub galley he had ever been in, with a faint, faint smell of frying onions hanging in the air no matter how many times that air went through the scrubbers.) Even this non-detailed version of the Grand Tour took Nathan a good while. As he went, the tiny creaks and movements of the boat around him, different-sounding though they were from subs he had been in before, told Nathan that she was moving fast and slowly coming deep; a few thousand feet now, perhaps, heading away from the precipitous underwater mountains of the Hawaiian Chain toward the deep basin between them and the Line Islands Chain in mid-Pacific. He found it difficult to tear himself away from his exploration of the space around him, but at the same time, the thought of the Bridge again, of a look out into the dimness of the great depths, lured him. Time enough to catch that launch. Later . . .

He headed forward again, through the starboard longitudinal corridor. Crewpeople were still staring at him as he passed, but Nathan had no eyes for them, seeing the flash of silver-blue come down toward him along the tube that ran down through the corridor, under its floor. The sleek shape paused in mid-corridor, looking sideways up at him. *I still can't get over it*, Bridger thought, and knelt a moment to tap 'hello' on the glass. Darwin gazed at him, rolled in the water, then flourished his tail and swam away to starboard, spiraling, obviously in high spirits. 'At least one of us is having a good time,' Nathan said softly, and stood up, shaking his head. A crewman passing glanced at him: Nathan indicated the dolphin, and said, 'Isn't that something?'

'Yessir,' said the crewman, sounding as if it wasn't something at all, and he went on his way. *Then again*, Nathan thought, as he ambled forward, shaking his head, *I guess they're all pretty much used to it at this point* . . . He found himself wondering about previous dolphin crew that the boat might have had: how many of them? And where were they now? Odd that none of them should have been on *seaQuest*, since she was ready to sail.

Unless, of course, Noyce had already known about one particular dolphin – and had removed whatever other dolphin crew there were in its favor –

Nathan shook his head at himself. *Paranoia? Or just healthy suspicion? ...* All the same, it was a pity. He had often worried, on the island, that 'Darwin didn't get out enough,' didn't see many other dolphins, due to his hanging around the island and working with Nathan. It would have been nice if there had been other dolphins here for him to talk to, creatures that didn't need a translator ...

I can't believe this, Nathan thought then. *I'm worrying about a cetacean's social life.* He made a wry face at himself and continued forward, pausing at one of the wallmounted 'status' panels, slipping his bifocals onto his nose and peering at the settings – they had defaulted to internal pressure and temperature, external pressure and temperature, bathymetrics – all very efficient. He turned away and ambled on toward the Bridge again. Ford caught up with him from behind, and fell into step next to him.

'Sir, we just received this message for you,' he said, holding out a note. 'I think it's from Admiral Noyce.'

Nathan resurrected the image of Noyce with a gallon ice-cream carton stuffed down over his head, and took the note, opened it, read it, then laughed softly.

'Good news?' Ford said.

Nathan laughed again. 'The Admiral was wondering if, while I'm aboard, I might take a look at the main drive propulsion unit. Seems there've been some "glitches" in the aqua-return jets.' He stuffed the note in his pocket. 'And here I was thinking that press-gangs had gone out of style. All the same – the glitches are to be expected. The old girl's been sitting with her feet up for eleven months:

this would be when the bugs would naturally come out of the woodwork.'

Ford nodded. 'Does this mean the Captain won't be returning to the mainland as planned?' he said.

'You can't wait to get me off this boat, can you?' Nathan said, amused.

Ford looked shocked. 'No, sir, I just –'

'It's all right, Commander. I'd probably feel the same if I was in your shoes. I assure you, I have no intention of snaking your command.'

'Snaking, sir?' Ford's expression was blank: almost carefully blank.

Nathan raised his eyebrows. 'Come on ... you're not saying that you don't believe this boat should be yours, are you?'

'No, sir,' Ford said, very calmly. 'I'm not saying that at all. But the fact is, those decisions are out of my control.'

Bridger looked at him for a moment. 'I guess you're right,' he said finally. 'I just want you to know that whatever it is Noyce has in mind, well, it isn't going to work.'

'Yes, sir,' Ford said: that calm tone again. 'Does that mean the Captain is ready to leave the *seaQuest*?'

Bridger glanced over at the tube: Darwin was back again, curious, he supposed: eavesdropping? Who knew what kind of attitudes a dolphin might have about privacy? Of course, now he could *ask* ...

'In good time,' Nathan said, a single answer to both Ford's question and his own.

And from down the hall, a voice shouted, 'Commander! Commander Ford!'

'Oh *no* ...' Ford turned around with the expression of

a man presented with one more problem he desperately doesn't want. Nathan shut his mouth and waited to see what happened: in the middle of his own annoyance, he was beginning, in a cockeyed way, to enjoy Ford's discomfiture.

The woman coming toward them now was wearing a science-team uniform: a handsome lady in her mid-forties, very brisk, very businesslike, and at the moment, from the look of her face, very angry indeed. She shouldered past Nathan as if he wasn't there, put her face right up to Ford's, and said, 'That's it! Enough! Let's get something clear, shall we? My people will not be treated like so much – *cargo*! *We* are scientists, capable of independent thought – not some mindless military drones –'

Ford didn't give an inch: his eyes narrowed, and right back into the woman scientist's face, he said, 'Your point, Doctor?'

'Your people have occupied areas clearly designated as research laboratories. I want them removed immediately!'

'May I remind you, *Doctor*, that you are aboard a military vessel. And your *orders* are to –'

The woman's eyes flashed scorn. 'Orders?? I don't take *orders*! This is a *research and exploration* vessel. We outnumber you. One hundred and twenty-four to eighty-eight.'

'That sounds like a threat.'

'Well, at least you have a grasp of the obvious!'

'Understand this –'

'Don't you point your finger at me –!'

Nathan couldn't keep it in any longer. He had been watching in silent hilarity up until now, but that last bit of business broke the dam. He started to laugh – and immediately the scientist whirled on him, discarding her old argument in favor of a refreshing new one. 'You find this amusing?'

'As a matter of fact, I do.' Though he tried to make it stop, the laughter kept coming back. 'How does anybody expect a lasting world peace when your two *teams* can't even agree on anything?'

The woman looked Nathan slowly up and down, not bothering to hide her scorn that this scruffy character should venture such an opinion. *I'm getting tired of this reaction*, Nathan thought ruefully, *I'm really going to have to do something* ...

'What are you,' she demanded, 'some kind of stowaway?'

'My name's Bridger.'

That worked, at least, because the sarcasm went away as if someone had flicked a switch. She looked most acceptably taken aback. 'You're ... *Nathan* Bridger?'

Nathan nodded. 'Last time I checked.'

The woman shook her head slowly, a thoughtful expression taking the place of the astonishment. 'I ... I know your work. Topography and thermal range variances, right? I've read your data ... from that island of yours in the Yucatan.'

Nathan allowed himself a quick smirk. He never had been sure how much of his material was making it out into the research community: after all, once the rumor gets around that you're behaving oddly, people sometimes begin to call your findings into question, on the grounds that your 'mental state' might be contaminating them. 'Was it helpful?'

'Very,' she said. 'I tried to contact you once. They said you were ...' She paused, hunting for some neutral word, as her eyes dwelt on him with a curious expression.

'... Unreachable.' Nathan had nothing to say to that for the moment. 'I'm Kristin Westphalen,' the woman said after a second. 'Medical doctor, physical oceanographer, and head of the science team aboard this ship.'

'Doctor,' Nathan acknowledged, looking at her as he extended his hand. He knew her work as well: hers was an incisive mind, but from the tone of her papers, a humorous one, a mind that considered no fact too small for interested investigation, no problem too big to attack. The entire military establishment of the UEO, for instance. There were traces of that humor and interest in her face, as well as a toughness that surpassed what he might have expected –

– and then he noticed that though the handshake had stopped, she was still studying him; no, eyeing him in a way he hadn't seen for a long time. He began wondering what she was looking at, now that she had got past the 'beachcomber' level. Deliberately he glanced away –

Westphalen broke the glance as well. 'Yes, well, I'm late for a staff meeting. It was – nice – meeting you.' She wheeled on Ford again, getting back to business. 'I'm not finished with this, Commander – not by a long shot!'

She turned and walked away.

They looked after her. Nathan was just as glad that anger hadn't been turned on him. At close range, it was like a typhoon: violent, but impressive. 'She seems very – committed,' he said to Ford.

The Commander snorted. 'She oughta *be* committed,' he said finally. 'Sir –' He nodded to Bridger and took himself away, looking decidedly hot under the collar.

Nathan smiled slightly. It had been a pleasant change to see someone besides himself thrown for a loop. Very pleasant indeed. He glanced at where Westphalen had been standing, raised his eyes towards where she had stalked off so full of righteous wrath, then smiled again, and went about his explorations.

*

The darkness at almost five thousand feet down is nearly total, broken only sporadically by the natural luminescence of the fish and invertebrates passing by. But there are other sources of light, even down that far, scattered here and there in the great depths.

Gedrick Power Station was one of these: a huge facility, spread for miles along the ocean floor over the crust of lava and sand and manganese nodules. At the core of the whole installation stood its central heat exchanger complex, set over the station's main geothermal source, a huge crack in the ocean floor through which, originally, gases and superheated water from the volcanic flow underneath it had vented freely into the open sea.

That energy was free and unlimited. Since there was no point in wasting it, the biggest gas-venting crack, buried between two half-mile-long lips of old pillow lava, had been blasted more or less level, its edges sealed with nustone and the remaining main opening capped. Then the drive and exchanger column had been built, a fairly standard turbine arrangement first driven by the pressure of the upward-jetting gases, then extracting heat from the gases after their pressure was exhausted. Other cracks, smaller, had their own vent towers built and sealed to them, and their gases were channeled to the main exchanger column, since the pressure they generated was usually negligible.

Shortly thereafter had come the storage tanks to hold the gas for processing – when cooled, it yielded sulfur and some hydrocarbons, again, too good to waste when nature was giving them away – and then more tanks were added to hold the liquids and gases which remained after the processing, both the valuable byproducts and the removable toxic and semitoxic wastes.

All around the main vent, the smaller vent towers of the power station speared upward into the crushing dark; they studded the web of piping that led to the storage tanks, and the industrial buildings that accessed and serviced them – offices, living quarters for the staff and the maintenance crews and their families. The connecting lacework of conduits was of incredible complexity, sheafs of pipes of all shapes and sizes twining among one another, weaving in every direction. Yellow lights glittered through the deep water, delineating the structures and piping. In an earlier day, the power station might have been mistaken for one of the huge petroleum-processing plants of North America's west coast. Such places were no more, though: this facility was their inheritor, cleaner, safer, tapping a form of energy easier to find and far more inexhaustible. Hundreds of stations like it were scattered across the bottoms of the world's oceans, the unseen foundation of the technological and power needs of the new century.

*

Other forces moved in those depths, equally unseen. The darkness sheltered the huge blunt cudgel-shape that moved softly through it, a shape of the previous century, but deadly for all its age. With its reactors shut down and its electrical crawl drive producing only enough turns for a slow, silent approach, the *Delta-IV* studied its prey.

The layout of Gedrick Power Station was spread out like a map on one of its sensor screens, glittering with different kinds of light: lines showing where the hot and cool gases ran, the paths of power conduits, and the great swell of geothermal heat beneath it all, a dull red like the color behind closed eyes.

The crewman bent over the display had eyes for nothing else at the moment. Marilyn Stark paced her cramped dark Bridge and ignored the display, considering her options – for even as easy an operation as this carried with it the possibility of so many things that might go wrong. Spend a while preparing yourself for every imaginable contingency, have your answers ready for the disaster that might happen ... and you would come through it on top regardless. Neglect even one possibility, and disaster threatened. Stark paced, thought, frowned.

Maxwell came to her, quietly, not wanting to break her calm: he had seen that happen, occasionally, and it was not something you brought on willingly, not if you wanted peace for the next few days. 'We're approaching Gedrick Power Station, Captain,' he said, and waited for any orders.

She nodded, said nothing: merely glanced at Maxwell, wondering how far into her confidence she might dare to take him. With this crew in particular she never unburdened herself too far: her last crew had been a good indication of how mistaken one might be to trust too completely, to let the others know what you were really thinking. Even with Maxwell, the only loyal one, the only one who had so far proved trustworthy ... even to him she could not always tell everything. That little voice in the back of her head warned her against confidences, against letting any other human being know too much of her mind. There was always the chance of betrayal, and it was most painful when it came from someone you had made the mistake of trusting ...

A sudden lurching blur of motion to one side alerted her, brought her around. It was Pollack, the aft Weapons-Control Officer – if officer was the word she was looking for: a big, blunt-faced, blundering type, who lumbered around the boat like a drunken bull, literally throwing his weight around in an attempt to dominate the others. *A pirate all right*, Stark thought regretfully as the man came up to her. *But a pirate from the old days. Not officer material by half.* One of the disadvantages of going ... independent ... as she had done, was that the available personnel tended to be of much lower quality than she would otherwise have ever tolerated. But it was an occupational hazard of this situation, and one you allowed for. There was, after all, a job to be done, and nothing could be allowed to interfere with *that* ...

Pollack came up now and stood close to her, too close: Stark's nose wrinkled. 'I don't get it,' Pollack said. 'Why do you have us attacking *this* power station?'

'It's strategic,' Stark said rather wearily. If he didn't get the point already, there was hardly any point in explaining it to him again.

'To what? We've got all the fuel we can carry! They haven't got anything worth taking! We should be –'

His head whipped back and around as Stark struck him across the face. He yelped. *As if you get a vote, you toad*, Stark

60

thought with satisfaction as Pollack reeled back from the blow, then staggered forward again, clutching his face, his eyes still tearing with the pain of the focussed strike. Rage was twisting that face now, as he towered over her, but Stark wasn't even slightly concerned about that – she knew quite well that if she had to, she could break him in two. She stared coldly at him.

'Don't *ever* question my orders,' Stark said, low, and let it sink in a moment. 'As long as *seaQuest* is out there, you people will never have the respect you need to be dealt with by the world community. I'll destroy her – but on my own terms.'

Pollack looked at her with utter hatred. Stark held his eyes, held them until Pollack couldn't bear it any more, and broke the gaze. He turned and lurched away again, not even cursing under his breath, and sat down hard in his chair again, glaring at his console screen.

Stark looked around the Bridge, waiting to see if anyone else thought this was a democracy, in which they were entitled to a vote. She almost wished they would – sometimes two lessons, one after another, worked better than one. But all around the Bridge, eyes that had been raised to watch what Pollack would do were now hastily lowered again to instrument panels. Stark didn't bother to smile. *No spirit*, she thought. *A pity to have to work with such poor material . . .*

She went back to her pacing for a moment or two, letting the Bridge go back to normal around her. After a few moments, 'What's the population of the power station?' Stark said casually to Maxwell.

He didn't have to check a readout: he knew, which was just as well for him. 'Fifty-nine workers. And their families.

One hundred and twenty-seven men, women and children all together.'

She nodded. 'Perfect. Set a new heading and disengage silent running.'

Then she waited, for there was a sort of pleading look in Maxwell's eye. Stark had seen it once or twice before, and had tolerated it ... as long as it didn't grow into anything like insubordination. This was the problem of having even one really good man on the boat, of course: the good were too often weak. They bent under stress, and broke at the test, in unpredictable directions. She watched Maxwell, now, to see which way he would break.

'Captain,' he said, 'if we resume normal power, *seaQuest* will know we're here.'

She looked at him. 'Before we're done,' she said, 'the whole world will know we're here.'

He drew near, near enough so that only she could hear him. 'Are you sure this is the only way, Captain?' he said, very softly, and the plea was in his voice now, too. 'Maybe we could –'

'No,' she said, quickly – before he could say something that would bring her to wonder whether he was any more use to her, really, than Pollack. 'In war there are no innocents.'

Silent now, his face unmoving, Maxwell turned away and went back to his duties. Stark looked after him, for just a moment, with the slightest regret that he really couldn't see it by himself: that he had to be *told* they were at war. It was the great difference, and always would be, between an officer like him and a commander like her.

Stark paced in the dimness, thinking, waiting for the moment to act.

*

The Bridge was hopping when he got there: twice as many crewmen seemed to be in it as had seemed to be there at any earlier time, and Nathan was glad once again of the roominess ... for otherwise the place would have been a zoo. There was no thinking straight when other people were getting in each other's way and stepping on your corns while getting to and from their stations.

He looked around and saw Ford and Hitchcock at the Communications Bay. O'Neill was seated before the console, monitoring his headset intently while the two senior officers hung over him and watched.

Nathan joined them, nodding to each. 'You wanted to see me, Mr Ford?'

Ford glanced sideways only briefly, unwilling to take his eyes off the board for long. 'We've got a distress call coming in.'

'Why are you telling me?'

Ford looked at him. 'UEO regulations require me to inform the ranking officer aboard of any emergency situations. That would be *you* –'

He went back to what he had been doing, with an air of a man disposing of an unnecessary chore. Bridger hesitated – then his curiosity got the better of him: he moved to follow Ford to O'Neill's station. 'What's the source of the call?'

Ford looked over at him, then said, 'Gedrick Power Station. It's apparently under some kind of attack. Aggressor unknown.'

'The signal is weakening,' O'Neill said, his eyes narrowing with concern. 'From the sound of it, the station's defenses – what minimal defenses they've got – have been blown to

63

hell. They're reporting numerous casualties, sir. And the attack is still going on.'

Hitchcock looked over at Ford. 'This could be the *seaQuest*'s first engagement under UEO command. Maybe you should contact Pearl for specific orders before –'

O'Neill shook his head. 'No can do, Lieutenant. We're too deep for rapid direct communication, sir.'

'How far to the nearest comms repeater buoy?' said Ford.

O'Neill checked his instruments, frowned, and Nathan heard the Comms chief swear softly under his breath. 'Almost five hundred kilometers in the opposite direction. It's a long detour.'

Bridger leaned in to have a look at the readouts on the comms panel, much more interested in their implications than in the political situation. 'What's our proximity to the station?' he said.

O'Neill glanced at Ford: Ford nodded at him. He said, 'It's on a border – part of the Gedrick Territory. Distance, forty-eight kilometers – depth, forty-nine hundred.'

Nathan did the math in his head, twice to be sure. 'With these currents, we could be there in twenty minutes.'

Ford took a deep breath, so loud – at least to Nathan beside him – that it was more like a gasp than anything else: but still Ford's face kept itself quite calm and still. He turned toward Nathan, standing curiously straight, a formal pose. 'Captain,' he said, 'I'm prepared to offer you command of the *seaQuest* at this time.'

'What ...?' Bridger heard the edge in Hitchcock's voice, and saw the hastily-concealed expression which crossed her face – serious doubt, mostly, tinged with unease for Ford's sake. He did his best to ignore it, at least for the moment, and straightened up from his examination of the readouts, also ignoring O'Neill's shocked look as he came by it on the way up.

'Come again?' he said.

Ford hesitated slightly. 'I was just wondering if the Captain would care to assume command at this time?' the man repeated.

The whole Bridge was looking at them now, waiting to see what happened. *What must it cost a man to make such an offer,* Nathan thought, *either willingly or unwillingly?* For a moment he was busy again with thoughts of what he was going to do to Noyce when he got off this forsaken tub: something lingering, with molten lead or boiling oil. *But that can wait. Meanwhile, I'm not going to impair Ford's efficiency with his people, not when he's trained with them, worked with them so long –*

He did the only thing he could think of to relieve the tension: he began to laugh. Shocked expressions were exchanged: plainly no one on the Bridge had expected *that* reaction. 'I'm sorry,' he said. 'You caught me by surprise.' He eyed Ford for a moment, then said, 'You don't strike me as the kind of officer to turn tail at the first need for a command decision, Commander.' He made a wry face. 'I think I know whose orders you're operating under. And if he were standing here right now, I'd punch his headlights out – for *both* of us.'

It wasn't enough: everyone in the Bridge was still standing too quiet, and they had no time now for such distractions. 'The answer is *no*, Commander,' Nathan said, more audibly. 'I'm just along for the ride. You're the man in charge.'

The small shifting sounds from all over the Bridge,

of people letting out held breaths, were noticeable. Bridger let out one of his own as he watched Ford's face. His feelings were horribly complex: out of the corner of his eye, he could see Crocker looking at him, disappointed. The look hurt him a little, but he could not afford to let it bother him. *To command again – But not under circumstances like these. To take a youngster's first command off him just because Bill Noyce thought it might massage my ego – No way.*

Ford hadn't yet looked away; he seemed to be studying Nathan's face for something. Nathan let him have his moment, wondering what Ford was looking for. *Cowardice?* A hard word, but possible. He understood how a man might suspect such in another who had run away from the 'real world' for seven years and had suddenly been pressured back into it. Unwillingness he might certainly expect to see. Fear would not surprise him either – and Nathan wouldn't deny it –

Ford turned away, toward O'Neill. 'Feed spatial coordinates of the power station to Navigation,' he said. 'Navigation, plot a new course, direct bearing! Helm and all other stations: prepare for incoming change of course and speed!'

Crewpeople started going about their business in the Bridge at some speed, almost as if they welcomed the relief of those few moments of tension, or the new sense of urgency. Bridger watched it all and found himself feeling slightly wistful: every one of them with a job to do, every one of them doing it, as they'd clearly done it before, separately, and now together. *As if they need you,* said the back of his mind to him, scornful, but pleased. He had plainly done the right thing. The crew hadn't needed him yesterday to do their jobs, and they didn't need him today. *Any more than I need them,* he thought.

But somehow, the thought didn't make Nathan feel any better.

The boat began to lean into her turn, changing course in a hurry. Nathan took himself out of the Bridge, and was not surprised when, looking back from the doorway, he saw that no one had noticed.

*

On the sea deck, the water was sloshing around to port, splashing up past the moon-pool coping and over the floors. Nathan stood watching this, soothed out of thought for the moment by the soft repetitive noise of it.

After a few sloshes, Darwin appeared in the pool, broke surface, and tail-balanced upward and out of it, looking at Nathan. He chattered, and in an interested tone of voice, the computer said, 'What – happening?'

'We're making a turn,' Bridger said.

Darwin slipped down into the water again, eyeing Nathan. '*We* – turn? Don't understand.'

'The ship – this cave we're in ...' He took a breath, wondering how to start making it clear. Propulsion systems, shipbuilding, underwater research, peacekeeping – but where do you begin with a creature that has always – literally – shifted for itself? *It would have been easier if he'd asked me 'what is truth?': then I could have gone off and washed my hands* ... 'I'll explain it later,' Nathan said, feeling extremely lame.

'*Much* to explain later,' Darwin said. There was a definite sound of amusement to the voice: Nathan suspected

Darwin knew how confused he was, and was enjoying the shift of roles.

'Yeah,' Nathan said. 'Much ...' And the sooner he started, he thought, the better – for Darwin's future life, it seemed, was going to be much fuller than it had been up until now. *Darwin play here,* the dolphin had said. What would Darwin do when Nathan told him that this was only a twenty-four hour ride, that he was going back to the island now, and said, come on, Darwin, let's go home?

Surely he would want to stay here – and Nathan's heart ached a little at that, but he couldn't imagine any other outcome at the moment. If a friend of *his* had suddenly caused him to be introduced to a fascinating alien culture, full of advanced technology – including a technology that made real communications with another species possible – and then, a day later, after letting him taste the wonders of the new world, said, 'Come on, let's go home' – Bridger knew perfectly well what *he* would have said, friend or no friend.

How could it be otherwise for Darwin? For this place plainly fascinated him, and Nathan couldn't let his own wishes interfere with what Darwin would certainly want, and what would in the long run be better for him. He had always known that the dolphin was extremely intelligent, but the relationship had always been a sort of more complex man-and-dog relationship, Nathan taking the lead, suggesting courses of action, and Darwin cooperating. Now, thanks to the translator technology, the fin was on the other foot, as it were. Or flipper. Darwin could make his own wishes known – and had. Why should he want to go back to being a 'dog', responding to hand signals, fetching rock samples, and listening to Nathan's monologues, when he could have *this* life – answering and asking, finding things out?

Something else to give Bill Noyce hell about, Nathan thought sadly: *the end of a beautiful friendship.* He looked at the pool again: Darwin was leaning his head on the coping, looking gazing thoughtfully at Nathan.

'Darwin,' he said –

Something went *splat* in the water, near them, spraying Nathan slightly: he and Darwin looked over at it in joint confusion. It was a bright-colored, many-sided water toy, an inflatable floating geodesic, made of the kind of durable plastic that suggested its designer knew it would be played with by members of a species with sharp teeth. 'Hey, fish breath!'

Darwin and Bridger looked up together. Lucas was standing there by the pool, now with a jacket over his flannel shirt, a jacket over-blazoned with a noisily clashing collection of mission patches, some of them well-loved and much-used antiques, by the smudged and ragged look of them – among others, he recognized the original *Challenger* patch, without the black band, and next to it, an ancient Soviet Frontal Aviation patch. It was a bizarre conjunction at best. What looked like an equally much-used portable 'notebook' computer was slung over the boy's shoulder by a strap. Darwin chattered loudly at the sight of him, and the computer translator said, delightedly, 'Lucas!'

The boy grinned with equal delight. 'I brought you that to mess around with. A gift.'

'*Gift?*' The dolphin slipped down into the water and smacked the surface of it with his chin, a gesture Nathan had occasionally seen him use to indicate confusion.

Lucas's eyebrows went up. 'Yeah. You don't understand "gift"? You should: it ought to be in the database ...' He unslung the portable computer, went over to one of the many instrument consoles around the sides of the room, plugged the computer into it, and began tapping briefly at the portable's keyboard. 'How about that?' he said, 'it's not in there. Wonder where it went? Well, hang on: I can fix it.' He went on typing, frowning occasionally, his face relaxing afterwards, as if a problem were being solved to his satisfaction. After a minute or so of this, when the boy looked up for a moment to let the computer do some piece of processing work, Nathan's presence in the room apparently fully registered itself: the boy looked up and nodded to him. 'How's it goin'?'

Nathan nodded back and sat watching. He was still dealing with his own reaction to the boy's smugness, and with some slight jealousy: but at the same time, a kind of creeping fascination was growing in him. Here was a fourteen-year-old who had managed something that Nathan hadn't after years of research. There might be something to be learned from him –

He watched Lucas work. Whatever else he might be, the boy was a demon typist, never once glancing at the keyboard, only at the screen above the input plugs. Nathan felt an uncharacteristic twinge of envy: every time he had approached anything like even half that speed, it always seemed that his fingers got terminally confused and started making a mess of whatever he was doing. But Lucas was having no such problems.

'Must have missed something in the last noun-syntax load,' he muttered, seemingly oblivious of Nathan's curiosity. 'Or else there was some kind of conflict with the irregular adverb-batching utility when that last vocabulary load went in. It happens. ...' After a few seconds more, he finished his inputting with a conscious flourish like a concert pianist's. Then he looked over his shoulder at the pool, and at Darwin, who was watching him.

'Okay, Darwin,' Lucas said. 'The word is *gift*. That toy is my *gift* to you.'

The dolphin listened to his side of the computer's translation. 'Gift,' he said after a moment. 'Okay. Thing given – nothing expected back.' Darwin flirted his tail, spinning himself to lie upside down near the surface. 'Darwin – play it now?'

'Play *with* it.'

'*With*,' Darwin said, slapping his tail on the water with impatience.

Lucas grinned. 'Yeah – go crazy.'

The dolphin eyed him. ' "Go crazy"?'

'*Play*. Go play.'

Darwin swam off in a burst of pleased speed, nosed the toy up from underneath, flipped it, caught it, then took it underwater with him. Lucas watched for a moment, satisfied, then turned to pop his portable's access plug out of the console.

He's awful friendly with my dolphin, Nathan thought – then took back that thought in embarrassment, already having guilt pangs about having called Darwin 'his' once today already, even in protective mode. Darwin was another intelligence: Nathan would no more want to own him than he would want to own another human being. And he was beginning to suspect that Darwin would have his own ideas about the subject ... which he definitely wanted time to discuss with him in detail before they had to part company.

Nathan sorted through a couple of possible openings, and then settled for the most innocent one. 'How long did that program take you?'

Lucas looked at him, somewhat surprised, then grinned. 'I'm not done with it yet. You saw.'

'The core code, I mean.'

'About a year ... The self-sampling part was the hardest. Six months for that alone.'

'How many lines?'

'Ninety-thousand odd. Haven't counted lately.' Lucas got a sudden wry expression. 'Not all error-free ...'

'Is a program ever?' Nathan said. He could remember his frustration with his own routines.

'Nope.' Lucas finished packing up his console. 'But worth it, I guess ...' He gestured with his head at Darwin, playing with his new toy, and the wry expression turned suddenly gentle. 'It helps havin' someone to talk to who doesn't ride me all the time. "Clean yourself up,"' he mimicked sarcastically, '"get a haircut, take your nose out of that book, stand up straight" –'

Nathan lifted one eyebrow a notch and said mildly, 'The haircut might not be a bad idea.'

Lucas snorted and eyed him with derision. 'Get one yourself first,' he said, and hand-signaled, *See ya round!* – then whisked out of the room, looking insufferably pleased with himself.

'Talking dolphins,' Nathan said softly. Darwin, perhaps thinking that he had been addressed, put his head up out of the water: then finding that he had not, took himself and his toy off under the surface again. '*Kids*. What else is going to turn up here? ...'

Something moved by the hatchway into the room, quite

low down: something pink. Bridger looked at it in surprise. At first he thought it was another toy – some kind of fuzzy plaything for someone's, as far as he knew, three-year-old. Then he saw that the fuzzy pink thing was looking *back* at him, out of two beady black little eyes. The pink thing – a teacup-sized poodle, he now saw with complete shock – started barking at him, or yipping, rather: an interminable string of noisy, high-pitched yipping that ratcheted and echoed around the pool room fit to wake the dead.

Nathan stared. It seemed the only possible reaction.

A few seconds later, a dark-haired woman in a sciences uniform hurried in, scooped up the little creature and headed away again. 'Sorry ...' she said to Nathan: and to the poodle, receding, '*Naughty* Lucrezia, naughty little mummy's wuzzy, mustn't bark at the nice fishie, now he's not a fishie but a mammal of course, but never mind that, now you just come and have your nice dinner ...'

Nathan sat very still and started taking a quiet inventory of his sanity.

*

Elsewhere, quiet was not the order of the day.

Sea water under pressure transmits sound faster than air – nearly four times faster, depending on local temperatures – so that any ship nearby could have quickly heard, without too much trouble, the noises coming from near Gedrick Power Station. Not the usual benign rumbles of the sea bed, the long low groans familiar to those who routinely deal with geothermal underwater sites as plates and strata shift. These rumbles were more deadly, the compressed, shocking sounds of explosions at close range, of creaking, strained and shattering metalwork, of pressure containers losing containment under the bombardment of E-plasma torpedoes. The flashes of the torpedoes, like the flash of lightning before a thunderstorm entirely too close, preceded the explosions by no more than a second or so; then the sea floor, and everything on it, rocked.

The biggest of the power station's gas storage tanks already lay cracked open like an egg, its metal outer shell still sizzling with the residual electricity of the spent E-plasma charge that had destroyed it. Everywhere around it, bent towers and tubework bowed downward and outward like trees knocked flat by a meteor-strike. Another E-plasma torpedo came screaming in, found its target, went up in a blinding flash of decontained charge, and blew down another grove of pipes and tubing. And over the blasted grove, silent and huge, the black hunchbacked shape of the *Delta-IV* came gliding through the water, sowing the thunder and the lightning as she came.

On the submarine's shadowy Bridge, Marilyn Stark stood over her Fire Control Officer, watching his every move – quiet, but with the quiet of the cat watching the mouse, waiting patiently for it to do something interesting enough to provoke the claws to come down. The man was sweating bullets with the twinned tension of needing to do his job correctly, and having to do it under that silent, relentless regard. Around the Bridge, no one else would look at the two of them: everyone was afraid to do anything that would attract the Captain's attention.

The only one who moved was Maxwell, who stepped up beside Stark, though softly. His face was bathed in sweat. 'Captain!' he said. 'Message just in! There's been a response to the station's distress signal. *The seaQuest is on her way ...*'

Stark nodded, and smiled, a small private smile of satisfaction. *Not much longer*, she thought. *We will resolve this little ... difficulty ... in a very short time. Not short enough for me ... but I can be patient a little while longer.*

Off to one side, though, Pollack's head swung around. His face was twisted with panic.

'Steady, Mr Pollack,' said Stark quietly.

Steadiness was not on Pollack's menu at the moment. 'Captain, I beg you to reconsider! We can't stand up against that ... that monster!'

I am really going to have to do something about this creature, Stark thought. *He certainly came highly recommended for his abilities, but as far as discipline goes, he's a loss.* 'We can and we will,' Stark said. 'I told you before, it's the only way we can assure victory for the cause.'

'The cause?' Pollack said, and looked at her open-mouthed. 'This isn't about a cause! This is about revenge! Everybody knows you were Captain of the *seaQuest*! Everybody knows you were *removed* from command!'

'That's enough,' Stark said softly.

But he was plainly beyond hearing anything, including her tone of voice. 'All you want to do is even the score! And if it takes killing this whole crew, you're prepared to do it. Well, *I'm* not willing to be part of the sacrifice! I'm settin' a course outta here *now*!' He turned back to his panel and began frantically making changes in the settings: a hundred-eighty-degree turn, from the brief glance Stark got.

'Mr Pollack ...?' Stark said.

Something in the tone stopped him, brought him around

... just in time to see the stungun aimed at his chest. His eyes went wide – but not as wide as when the charge hit him. The blast of energy convulsed his muscles so that they, rather than the discharge itself, slammed him back against the console: he collapsed to the floor, mouth slack, eyes still open but now unseeing, limbs twitching as the residual traces of the stun-charge fired off randomly in his nerve-endings. All around, the crew stared, as horrified by Stark's calm stance as by Pollack's condition.

That suited Stark. 'I had one Lieutenant who counter-manded my orders once,' she said reflectively. 'I won't have another one ...' She glanced around.

'Is there anyone else who thinks they can run this boat better than me?' she said. The silence was profound. 'Well? Isn't there even *one* of you who wants to step forward and challenge *seaQuest*?'

Silence. Stark smiled. 'I didn't think so. If you want to win, I'll show you how: if you want to die, I can arrange that too. But don't *ever* question my orders.'

Once again everyone became abnormally interested in their instruments, preferring their bland mechanical regard to the chill look of threat in Stark's eyes.

'Set course, Mister Maxwell,' Stark said. 'Prepare to get underway.'

'Aye,' Maxwell said softly, and went about it.

Stark settled into her chair and stared out into the darkness.

FIVE

In the dimness, the WSKR probes plunged through the water at speed, one far out at the point, the other two spread wide to the flanks and coming hard after it. At this distance, the glow of the lights of Gedrick Station was showing only faintly – but that was no problem for the probes: light was only one of the data they worked with, and the lack of it hardly mattered.

On *seaQuest*'s Bridge, Bridger came in to find the place gone quick and tense with activity as they approached the station. Ford was standing behind the helmsmen, watching their coordinated efforts as they guided the huge submarine downward into Gedrick's little valley. The seabed was hardly flat here: as in other active volcanic areas, sudden spikes and hills of stone stood up apparently without rhyme or reason, thrust up by old eruptions, and an ever-present trouble for the unwary submariner. But *seaQuest*'s front screens were showing a 3-D side-looking sonar 'landscape', altering as they swept across it – as plain a landscape as the helmsmen might have seen above the water, under daylight; and they also had information from other sources.

'Whiskers are kicking back data now!' Ortiz called to Ford. 'One boat – a *Delta*.' The passive-energy indicator which showed the levels of output electromechanical energy in the area was dancing up near the top of its scale. 'She dished out one hell of a firestorm!'

Bridger's head turned sharply towards the sensor suite, trying to see more even before the probes updated their input. *Delta* – it was an ex-Soviet boomer, and with that length-to-beam ratio, the configuration was Type III or IV. Not quite the biggest boat they had ever floated, but big enough, and armed with a six-tube torpedo battery. Nasty. Very nasty.

A lot of those old subs had been decommissioned and sold off, and with their missile spaces cleared they fulfilled a variety of functions not envisioned by their original designers. Mining survey ships, or undersea research vessels of one sort or another: why go to the expense of building new when you could buy secondhand and refit? Or mobile and not-so-mobile homes; Nathan had heard of two old British Royal Navy *Vanguards* that had been anchored to the bottom and now formed the core of a thriving community. A community like the one this bastard was shooting up.

At least it wouldn't be especially manoeuvrable. Those things had been built for stealth and silence, not underwater dogfights like an *Alfa* or a 688 *Los Angeles*. *seaQuest* should be able to run rings around it, and the marauders had to know that. It wasn't as if the *seaQuest* was a secret any more. The raiders would likely turn tail as soon as they knew she was in the area – but knowing that she might be, as they must have done, why risk this attack in the first place ...? *Something else is going on,* Nathan said to himself. *Otherwise it just doesn't make sense ...*

'Power station communications is reporting major structural damage,' O'Neill said, working at his console to strengthen the incoming signal through the interference from the attack. 'Life support systems nominal. Surviving worker-residents are gathering in the main complex –'

Bridger stood there watching it all happen, feeling helpless and hating it. Ortiz looked up from his console and said sharply, 'Assault vessel is on the move, Commander! Heading ... two-zero-seven degrees, making turns for thirty knots. She's heading away from the station!'

Thirty? Dammit, that's five knots above specification. Somebody's been tweaking the turbines again ... Nathan's head turned immediately to the forward screens, but nothing showed there yet. Ford stepped up beside him. 'Give me eyes, Mr Ortiz ...'

It took a second. Then the screens came alive with the three separate views of the WSKR probes, annotated with bright telltales showing direction, distances and depths. In all of them, the renegade sub loomed, just clearing the outer perimeter lights of the power station, and heading slightly upward, in a leisurely fashion, for open water and the big rift beyond. A blunt-nosed cylinder of a hull, with an ominous-looking hump where a fish's dorsal fin would be, running two-thirds of the craft's length. It was a *Delta-IV*, that much was certain. Even under its refit – *and where the hell did they get* that *done?* Nathan asked himself grimly – the brute was unmistakeable. At least the *seaQuest* was bigger – but other matters remained to be proven ...

Ford stepped away from the center seat, leaving Nathan

standing there wondering what the man was doing. *Is he just going to leave us sitting here while that thing dances around us? If it gets an advantage –* 'Helm,' Nathan muttered under his breath, 'bring 'er around …'

Ford looked up then, though there was no sign that he had heard Bridger. 'Helm … bring her around, two-zero-seven, intercept course.'

'Coming around to intercept course,' the helmsman came in like an echo.

Ford's just a touch slow, Nathan thought, starting to get concerned. *No more than that. But at a time like this, it's enough to get us killed.* He shook his head, watching Hitchcock move to take Ford's position at the Ex-O's station. *That's the way,* Nathan thought. *For pity's sake, call battle stations, don't just stand there.* He tried to catch Hitchcock's eye, and enthusiastically mimed hitting one of the console controls. She didn't see him.

'Sound battle stations!' Ford said at last. Hitchcock did it, and the alarms went off, an eerie insistent noise that would have demanded instant attention even of a crew that wasn't already strung tight as the fifth string of a Strad. Elsewhere in the boat, Nathan could hear the sound of watertights thumping shut between sections, one after another: the Bridge's own doors shut themselves and sealed automatically.

'Targeting profile up!' Ford said. On the forward screens, the targeting grids came on, overlaying themselves on the Whisker's-eye views of the renegade sub and adjusting themselves to scale.

'Targeting grid locked!' Ortiz said.

'All ahead full,' Ford said. 'I want this one.'

No, no, no! Nathan thought, unable to stand it any more.

He stepped over to Ford, leaned over confidentially close to him, and said, 'Commander, a moment, please?'

'I'm a little busy –' *Too much going on, I don't have time for this*, said the Exec's expression.

He took Ford by the arm. *'Now*,' he said, and pulled him a little off to one side.

Bridger bent his head close to Ford's. 'I think there's a couple of things you want to consider here.'

'Such as …?'

'Such as the lives and safety of all those people at that power station.'

Ford shook his head. 'I'm aware of that, but if that sub gets loose, it'll be free to attack somewhere else …'

Nathan breathed out in exasperation that someone could have a situation so obvious in front of him and not see the key to it. 'If! You're talking hypotheticals! I'm talking reality!' He glanced around with an awkward realization of just how loudly that had come out, and saw heads turn back to their duties. Or at least, seem to …

'Look, you can take out the raider *after* you help those people.' He waved an arm around him. 'This boat's a thousand-foot-long Swiss army knife. *Use your options*. Have one of your Whiskers *tag* the bad guys. We –' he caught himself with a slightly sardonic look – 'uh, you – can always go after them later.'

Ford looked at Bridger, thinking. Nathan didn't so much as blink, afraid to disturb the man's train of thought while he weighed the options, because the only alternative was the unacceptable one of simply taking over command. Just the way Bill Noyce wanted him to do. A suspicion flickered at the back of his mind, then faded as a second later Ford nodded, opened his mouth. 'But the manual says –'

'Oh, forget the damn manual! Use your instincts. Your gut!' Nathan just barely restrained himself from catching Ford a good solid poke in the area under discussion. 'That's what separates the good from the great.'

Ford thought about it –

'Hey,' Crocker said, 'if anybody cares ... that boomer is makin' a turn ...'

All heads came quickly up to watch the screen. Sure enough, the heavy dark shape of the *Delta* was banking slowly around to starboard. Ortiz was watching his console with a worried frown: now he looked up. 'Target sub is coming around!' He looked over at Ford, alarmed. 'She's moving into an *attack* posture!'

Ford swallowed and stepped over into position by the Command chair. His shoulders actually looked a little bowed: Nathan looked at him with concern and some sympathy, knowing that crushed feeling, the very literal weight of command – the way it felt when it came down on you and you tried to make yourself equal to it – or to shrink down where it couldn't see you. Ford hit the in-ship comms button on the Command chair. 'Weapons room,' he said. 'Flood forward tubes! Prepare E-plasma torpedoes! Uh ... sixty percent charge.' *Why not a hundred? Nathan thought irritably. Who knows what kind of armor that thing had put in when they did the retrofit? Think, son –!* 'Helm – reverse engines, one-quarter, six degree down angle –'

'Reverse one-quarter, down six degrees ...'

Bridger stood there watching the other vessel in the front screens, and shook his head slightly. *Too shallow.* '*Eight* degrees –' he said behind his own clenched teeth. Then he compressed his lips in a grim smile: this kind of backseat driving was as bad for the passengers as for the driver.

Shut up and let him do it, Nathan. If you think you can do it better, you should have accepted his offer when you had the chance –

Hitchcock was watching her board like an eagle. 'Her forward tubes are flooded, bow caps coming open – all of 'em!'

Ford's dark skin was as close to ashen as it could get. *Not cowardice*, Nathan thought, almost with pity. *Just ... the first time ... when he had hopes that things would go so differently.* He kept silent and stood there, watching that grim shape on the screens ...

*

Inside the *Delta-IV* all was silent, except for the soft chirps and mutters of the various ranging and weapons systems reporting themselves ready, and the faraway rush of water, now diminishing, as the forward trim tanks countered the effect of the flooded torpedo tubes. Marilyn Stark leaned over two of her crewmen, intently watching the readings on their panels, watching the *seaQuest*, waiting to see what would happen.

The crewman to her right, the sensor chief, like his partner on the left, was covered with sweat at the sight of what was coming after them. 'Captain!' he said, his voice almost breaking – from the sound of it, he was as frightened of speaking as of what looked to be about to happen. 'That – "thing" is getting ready to fire! Shouldn't – shouldn't we take evasive action?'

Stark stood there and watched the readings, eyed the screen that gave her visuals. 'Impressive, isn't she ...' Stark said, admiring the sleek dark shape gliding through the water. Normally that shape would have inspired more than mere aesthetic pleasure, of course. Normally, an informed commander's thoughts would have turned immediately to her more important attributes: propulsion and weaponry ... especially the latter.

Stark smiled to herself. She had already given that last considerable thought, with the result that no more need now be given.

'Captain –!' the sensor chief said desperately.

Stark only kept smiling, and said nothing.

*

On *seaQuest*'s Bridge, Ford was still an unwholesome color, but this time Nathan thought there was better reason. They were staring at the helm station, and at readouts that were no longer making sense. 'What do you mean "not responding"?' Ford demanded.

'Helm control is frozen, sir!' The Helm Officer was another big man, from the same mould as Chief Crocker, but for all that his hands were leaping about over his controls with surprising speed and delicacy, the deft, sure motions of a specialist who knew the console forwards, backwards, and in the dark. 'She's not lettin' me take the reins!'

Ford swallowed. Nathan began to sweat. *He's not ready for this*, he thought. *Come on, son, think you can find your way around this one. Get Hitchcock onto this, if she can't figure out what the problem is then you* do *have trouble –*

But there shouldn't be *this kind of trouble in the first place! This boat is* new!

'Lieutenant,' Ford said to Hitchcock.

'On it, sir,' she said, and headed for the helm to check out the problem.

'Distance to target?' Ford said to Ortiz.

'Eight hundred meters and closing!'

Ford nodded. 'Open forward tubes! Prepare to fire!'

For some reason, Bridger found himself holding his breath. A moment later, he found out why.

'We can't, sir!' said Phillips, the Weapons Officer, sounding more angry at the failure of equipment than scared by its consequences. 'Weapons control isn't accepting our commands!'

Now this is ridiculous, Nathan thought, making his way again to stand beside Ford. *This thing's not two hours out of dock and it's falling to pieces!* He had begun sweating earlier, and this now started to get more pronounced – as much from embarrassment as anxiety. *This is my boat, my design, my creation – and now she's going to get me and everybody else aboard her killed!!*

'Go to redundant systems,' Ford said. His voice was beginning to acquire an edge of fear that Nathan didn't like. Not that it was wrong to feel fear, or to express it – but the expression had to be appropriate, and if it wasn't, it could spook a whole crew – with disastrous results.

'Redundant systems refuse to engage!' Hitchcock said, and there was fear in her voice too.

'What else can go wrong?' Ford said, and swallowed again. And that was all that Nathan had a chance to see, because a bare second later, all the lights on the Bridge went out. The light of the screens wavered, and then the displays came up again as their own independent power systems cut in. By their ghostly light, people could be seen staring at one another in horror and sheer astonishment.

Ortiz was staring, not at the other crewmen, but at his own display. 'Target vessel has just fired, sir!' he shouted. 'One electrostatic torpedo away – homing … Locked and heading in!'

Only one? Nathan thought. Though he was under fire again for the first time in years, he felt strangely calm – and very surprised. *Under the circumstances, maybe we should be grateful – but hey, aren't we supposed to be the new UEO supership? You'd think they'd at least fire a spread – unless they have some kind of idea that since we're a peacekeeper, we're not armed at all –*

There followed a second's breathless silence. Even when they locked on, E-plasma torpedoes sometimes failed to acquire their target properly – not that this failing necessarily solved your problems: sometimes it made them worse. But it had to be taken into consideration. *All right*, Nathan thought desperately, *it would have happened by now, and it hasn't –* he was right, they're locked on, dammit. *Countermeasures – come on, Commander! Countermeasures!*

'Countermeasures!' Ford shouted.

Hitchcock headed back for her station and started hitting switches. Nathan watched as she brought up the display of countermeasure routines – false plasma, EM misdirect, decoy echo return – and apparently decided not to be shy, but to call for all of them, wide spread, favoring forward –

And nothing happened. The blank spot in which the 'accept' statement should have immediately appeared just lay there black and empty.

'Countermeasures aren't responding –!' Hitchcock reported, furious. *What the bloody blue blazes is wrong with my boat?!* He watched her try a systems reroute, sourcing the countermeasure routines through the main computer's redundant backups. Nothing: the console just sat there, with the damned torpedo still on its way in and the shrill whine of its approach audible even through *seaQuest*'s hull –

'Sound collision!!' Ford said. It was all he could do. The collision klaxon started howling through the boat like a banshee. The front screens showed, all too clearly, the WSKRs' tripartite view of the E-plasma torpedo heading toward them, a spinning top carved out of malignant ball lightning that left a trail of expanding smoke-filled bubbles behind it as it literally burned the water into hydrogen and oxygen in its passing.

'Everybody hold tight!' Ford said. On the darkened Bridge, everyone grabbed something steady enough to serve as a handhold, and hung on, grimly waiting, counting the seconds. Bridger braced himself on the Ex-O's station, listening to the electrostatic whine scaling up and up, getting louder and louder as the torp plunged in at them –

– and hit, and everything rocked, all the images in all the screens whiting out, then rolling back in again, jittering with the power fluctuations. One of the WSKR probes' images in the main screens showed that the torpedo had hit just abaft the Docking Sphere and a searing blue webwork of plasma charge was crackling along *seaQuest*'s hull from the point of impact.

'Damage control!' Ford shouted.

Hitchcock had left the helm, obviously unable to make any headway with it, and was back at her engineering station, her hands swiftly manipulating the controls. 'Port side strike!' she said, and a look of pain twisted her face. 'Definite hull damage! We're taking on water!'

Nathan felt for her: she was clearly one of those

engineers who experienced a given ship as an extension of their body, and felt any damage to it like a wound. But he had other things to think about at the moment. Ford's face was a study in helplessness, wearing the expression of a man caught in his worst nightmare, and finding that there was no waking up from it: it was real. 'Where are my battle systems, Lieutenant?'

She shook her head, still working over the console, and looking angry as well as upset. 'Inoperable! All still down!'

'*Delta* is preparing to fire a second strike!' Ortiz said, and looked over at Ford.

Everyone was looking at Ford now, waiting for the answer, or at least for an order.

'Commander.' Bridger said. But Ford only stared at the screens: an order might be needed, but he was fresh out.

Bridger wasn't: he found, not entirely to his surprise, that adrenalin still speeded up more than just his reading speed. While waiting for that torpedo to hit, he had been watching the landscape on the forward screens, and had noted the dark shadow past the perimeters of the Gedrick station, blackness, a depth too deep for the side-looking sonar to fathom. Quickly Bridger stepped up beside Ford. 'Blow open all ballast tanks, fore and aft!' Bridger said.

The Bridge crew stared, understandably enough, and Ford looked at him, uncomprehending. Hitchcock stared, plainly wondering whether she was really supposed to listen to this beachcomber –

'Do it!' Bridger nearly shouted.

Hitchcock blinked, then touched the controls to bring up the ballast diagrams and menu, and vented the tanks, all of them – aft first to bring the stern up and let the bow angle down. There was an immediate whoosh as the neutral-buoyancy air left the tanks, and then an increasing roar as seawater flooded in to take its place. The deck slowly began to tilt. Backwards ...

Bridger quickly went to Ortiz's station, had a look at his screens, pointed at one of them. 'How deep is that rift below us?'

'*Deep*. Twenty-two thousand feet!'

The more the merrier, Bridger said to himself. *I think.* Ortiz was looking at him with a combination of bemusement and concern as Hitchcock called, 'We're into a crash dive!'

Nathan ignored her. 'Helm,' he snapped, 'take us into that hole!'

'Crash diving into a narrow rift with slow helm response –' The helmsman gave him an if-you-say-so expression. '*Sure*. I always wanted a burial at sea ...'

Nonetheless, he wore an edge of grin as he said it, and turned back to his console to carry out the order. Ford stepped over to Nathan and said softly, 'Captain, this boat wasn't designed for a crash dive.'

'You're tellin' *me*,' Nathan said. *Stupid of me to assume it wouldn't be necessary. Let's hope good materials and workmanship will save our asses now ...* 'If you've got a better idea, I'm wide open! Otherwise ...'

But Ford shook his head. There *was* no otherwise.

seaQuest sank into the rift, her stern a little lower than her bow despite all Nathan's efforts: the dive planes were out of angle, he suspected, because of the problems with the helm. The WSKR probes were now well up and out of the way, watching her sink, relaying the pictures of it: and of the *Delta*, plainly not ready to be cheated of a fight, plunging down into the rift after *seaQuest* at full power.

They fell. They fell. The creakings of the hull grew slowly louder: soft voices at first, then moans, long, odd, subdued howls, getting more and more frequent as the titanium-composite frame began to compact slightly under the increasing pressure. The readouts on first one of the main screens, then another, flicked out, and there was nothing to be done about it – the WSKRs' telemetry systems sometimes became finicky at the greater depths, and in a dive at speed like this, the signal would become deranged anyway. Bridger sighed and shook his head: the Whiskers would take care of themselves, holding at 'depth of last signal' until they got better or clearer instructions from Ortiz or the ship's computers: if they lost carrier entirely, they would store their data and make for the nearest relay buoy, then home on Pearl. If worst came to worst, at least the UEO would know what had happened to its pride and joy. *A lot of consolation it'll be to* us, Nathan thought sourly, and willed the boat, *his* boat, to hang on...

*

The commander of the pursuing submarine, though, heard no one willing anything. Her own will, and her whole attention, was concentrated on the screen image of the sleek dark shape which was preceeding her, slightly stern-first, downward into the abyss.

The sensor chief and all the crewpeople around him were doused with sweat, as if someone had upended buckets of it over them: the place reeked with their fear. 'Captain!' the sensor chief was saying, as he had said several times now, varying only the numbers he appended to his protests. 'Captain, *seaQuest* is heading down – into that rift. We can't follow, not in this ...!'

'Maintain pursuit. I don't care what she does, stay with her ...' Stark hadn't taken her eyes off the image in the screen, drifting downward, drifting away. *I will not let you get away,* she thought. *You got away from me once. Never again. And if I can't have you, no one will.*

The hull was howling protest, a noisy counterpoint to the mutterings of her crew. She ignored both interruptions and concentrated on the image in the screen.

'We should fire!' Pollack said.

'No,' Stark said, 'not yet. I want to get closer.'

Never again ...

*

'Eight thousand feet and dropping,' said Ortiz, forcing himself calm.

'Systems are crashing all over the boat ...' Hitchcock said, as the hull-groans got louder still. Nathan nodded, exchanged what was meant to be a reassuring glance with Ford – but Nathan felt, if truth were told, that he could use some reassurance himself at this point. Not that any was forthcoming.

The third screen's image was getting grainy with dive artifact and the failure of most of the image-processing systems: it was hard to make out much of anything on it.

'Where's our friend?' Nathan said to Ortiz.

'Still pursuing ...'

That hardly came as a surprise to Nathan. *That sub wanted us for some reason. Wanted us enough to attack a power station to draw us in.* He was convinced of it now: there was no other explanation. *Why? Why?*

'All right,' Nathan said, 'let's see how bad they want us. Take her to the bottom.'

Heads swiveled all around the Bridge, and everyone stared at him.

'Is there a problem?' he said.

'No, sir,' Ortiz said.

Nathan stepped up by Crocker in the number two helm seat, watching, impressed but concerned, as the big man muscled the helm controls over, trying to regain some kind of balance between the helm malfunction and the dreadful pressure of the water at these depths flowing over the dive planes *in the wrong direction.* He glanced up at Nathan.

'This mean you're Captain now?' he said, cheerfully enough.

Nathan gave him a dirty look, thinking, *No wonder you keep getting your stripes busted off. Later for you, you sonofa* – 'Just tryin' to save our necks, Chief. Just tryin' to save our necks...'

The slope of the dive increased: the boat moaned more loudly. They fell, and fell, and the *Delta* followed.

An old sub, Nathan thought. Only one careful owner. Well, *mostly* careful, except when the thing got its sail caught in someone's fishing nets and dragged them halfway across the Irish Sea backwards at fifty knots. Or was that an *Alfa?* Who cares. Bought second-hand from little old Mother Russia, who never used it except to cruise around the North Cape and maybe tiptoe up people's fjords without telling them. But, in any case, no matter what kind of armor these pirates have glued onto it, *old.* Maybe not real well maintained since it was converted: you just can't get the spares any more. And certainly not built for this kind of thing. He willed whatever conscienceless bastard was commanding the big black ugly brute to see reason, break it off, run away and play somewhere else before they were destroyed ...

... and before I find out for sure whether or not my baby can take this kind of strain ...!

Crocker had been smiling until he looked back at his controls. Then the smile fell off. 'Thirteen thousand,' he said.

Go away! Nathan willed whoever stood on the Bridge of that other sub, only faintly visible now on their screens. *Are you completely nuts? You think that poor caviar-can will stand these kinds of depths? You really want to kill all the poor slobs you're dragging around to do your dirty work? Who do you think you are, Captain Ahab or something? Because this boat's no white whale! What the hell kind of captain are you? Even the old-time pirates who braided firecrackers into their beards and set them off weren't this crazy –!*

seaQuest's hull moaned more and more loudly, beginning to sound like a beaten puppy as structures never meant to be subjected to such strain now began to bend and buckle under them. Nathan's heart bled for his creation. According to Noyce, she could go to twenty thousand feet. But backwards, with her hull integrity compromised, and in an uncontrolled crash dive? That was another story. He could not take his eyes off the screens, off the black shape that followed. The abyss was still a better chance ...

*

'We're almost at ten thousand feet,' Stark's sensor chief

muttered. 'We can't do this ...' He didn't care any more that she was right behind him, leaning over his seat, staring at the screen as if she was unable to tear her eyes from the image of *seaQuest*, still falling away before her. But not for long. And when they caught her –

'Maintain pursuit.'

'Captain!' Maxwell said from beside her. 'Captain!' She would not look away from the screen. 'You heard the man. *Ten thousand feet!*' Now it was nearly a shout in her ear: he was desperate. 'The retrofitted armor isn't going to hold any deeper – they wouldn't even guarantee us to ten! *Captain!*'

She could not look away from the screen. *They will not get away. Not again.*

Maxwell leaned close to her: not that she saw him do it – only that his voice came to her, not as a shout now, but almost a whisper, from right by her ear. 'If we let ourselves get crushed,' he said, '... the seaQuest *wins!*'

That caught her attention. The words clutched at Stark's heart like a fist, for if she died, there would be no chance for her revenge, ever again. Later, after it was achieved, and her family honor put right, she might die: but not before. Slowly, slowly, Stark looked up at him: and Maxwell gazed back at her, unmoving, waiting to see what she would do.

Waiting ...

*

Bridger hung onto the back of the helm chair and watched the black shape on the screen fall closer and closer toward them. The muttering on the Bridge had faded away to nothing in the face of the appalling determination of that other sub's commander. A deep dive was nothing to this boat, they all knew that. But damage from an E-plasma torpedo strike was exponentially increased by depth, and they had been hit once already, squarely amidships, the place where a strike was most difficult to isolate and control. One more, anywhere else, would be more than enough to finish them. Everybody was waiting for the sound that would not be a moan, but the screech of that second torpedo, and right after that, the inward crash of catastrophic implosion as the *seaQuest* blew herself in half ...

'Fourteen thousand, five,' Crocker said, sounding resigned, now, as if announcing a baseball score that he didn't particularly care about.

Nathan breathed in, breathed out again, wondering each time if this would be the last time he would get a chance to do it.

Then, 'She's going up!' Ortiz cried. 'Ten degrees – fifteen – The *Delta's* breaking off! She's moving away!'

There was a long moment of silence: no one quite dared believe it, everyone was a bit too numb to respond. Then people started letting out all *their* last breaths.

Bridger took another long one, and thought, *It just goes to show you: never let your hardware be built by the lowest bidder. I'm so glad I made them scrap the old tender system for this lady ...*

'Don't let her out of your sight, Mr Ortiz,' Nathan said. 'We don't want her doubling back on us.'

'Yes, Cap –' Ortiz stopped, '– uh, sir – uh, *yes* ...'

Nathan smiled. The feeling was so strange, after the tension of the last few minutes, that he thought his face might crack. He turned to Crocker, then. 'Chief – pump some oil into our ballast tanks. We gotta stop dropping like a stone.' He made a wry face. 'Who knows? We may even want to go *up* – and save those power station people.'

'Aye aye, *Skipper.*'

Oh God, Nathan thought, grimacing, and turned away.

He found Ford right in front of him, which was more or less the last thing he wanted at the moment, for Ford looked extremely uncomfortable, like a man who had to say something, but didn't know what. *It's mutual,* Nathan thought. 'That okay with you, Commander?' he said.

'Yes, sir. Check *Delta*'s positioning, Mr Ortiz. I don't want to get caught with my pants down again.' Then he turned back to Nathan.

'We'd better check out the damage,' Nathan said.

Ford nodded, accepting: but it was plain to Nathan from Ford's troubled look that something was bothering him ... and he didn't much want to deal with it. *It's not my table,* he thought.

As they headed out, though, Bridger had a feeling that eventually, it was going to be.

SIX

It took a while to climb up out of the abyss, and they spent a rather longer while hovering above Gedrick Power Station, surveying its damage, and their own. The station was the worse damaged. Designed before the advent of E-plasma torpedoes, it had no such defenses against them as *seaQuest* had, and large parts of the station lay dark and shattered now, the bright lights of the outbuildings and towers dimmed, or darkened entirely.

seaQuest herself had done well enough, despite the uncontrolled plunge. Under proper control, with all systems up and running, there would have been no problems; as Noyce had said, she had been tested far deeper. But not in a stern-first crash dive brought on by an emergency flooding of her main tanks, and doubly not while there was torpedo damage to her outer casing. While she lay over the station, standing guard over its evacuation, the WSKRs hovered outside the hull, scanning the place where the E-plasma torpedo had struck. There was an ugly, jagged scar there, some meters long, but it was now a closed scar, healed over: the homeostatic single-fibre hull, designed to repair

97

its own breaches, had done its job, sealing out all but the initial influx of water, and preventing catastrophic implosion. It had also isolated the transmission of the electrostatic charge, which, unconfined, would have wrought havoc with the on-board life-support and computer systems, possibly killing everyone inside more quickly than mere hull damage.

Shuttles had been coming and going for an hour now, bringing aboard the families from the station, taking *seaQuest* personnel over to help save what equipment could be saved, and to help shut down what was too complex or dangerous to move. The docking bay looked like an impromptu refugee camp: a dim one, for the boat was running on auxiliary power, and in the low glare of the emergency lighting stood a crowd of men and women and children, all wet, frightened, and cold, being helped by *seaQuest* crew with blankets and medical aid. The medical team had already partitioned off one area of the docking bay for triage: blanketed forms huddled or lay there, and the medics were moving hurriedly from one to another of them.

All the crewpeople around him were the picture of efficiency, and Bridger knew that everything which could be done was being done; but he still felt sorry for these poor station people, whose quiet lives had suddenly been shattered by renegades ... and for what? The answer to that one was still beyond him: the memory of that ruthless and implacable pursuit of *seaQuest* by the *Delta* still made him want to shudder. He still couldn't understand it. But in the meantime, *these* folks were suffering for what, to them, must seem no reason. Where would they go now? ... what would they do? ... – Nathan heard them asking each other the question, in tears sometimes, and wished he had some kind of answer.

The sound of tears reached him again and he glanced over to one side to see a small girl, near two lost-looking adults whom he suspected were her parents. The child was standing by her small self, crying, grinding her little fists into her eyes. He saw the father look down, his hands and arms already full with a bitterly weeping wife, and simply not be able to cope; he buried his face in his wife's shoulder, just not wanting to see.

Bridger went over to the little girl, hunkered down in front of her, took those small hands away from her face, and wiped her eyes, wondering what to say to comfort someone this small. Finally, at a loss, 'Tell me something,' Nathan said. 'Have you ever talked with a dolphin? ...'

Very big-eyed, sniffing, but not sniffing nearly as hard as she had been, she shook her head. Nathan picked her up.

O'Neill was not far away, working on one of the wall panels. He leaned in toward Nathan and said, very softly, 'Sir ... uh, I believe that particular project is *very* top secret ...'

'Huh,' Nathan said, and walked off with the little one toward the sea deck.

*

It was a good while later before Nathan found time to make his way down to the engine room. The place was now nine-tenths drained of the water which had come rushing in from the torpedo strike – and that torp had been entirely too cannily aimed: Nathan found himself wondering exactly how it was that the *Delta*'s commander

99

had known where to put a single shot to best advantage. *Too damn effective*, he thought, looking around at the dripping walls and ceiling. The damage crews were still busy welding and patching the inflexible inner hull and its struts and bulkheads, vacuuming the water out of the 'tween-hulls space, and adding more 'memory' compound to the exterior hull, in the places where it was exposed, to help rejuvenate the polymer weave where it had been damaged by the torpedo. Others were busy trying to salvage the soaked electronic equipment: besides the usual hygroscopic 'drying' foam, someone had brought in buckets of fresh water to get rid of surface brine, and portable battery-powered hairdryers were much in evidence, nothing better having yet been invented for the drying-out of wet chips and system boards. Panels the damage control people hadn't yet gotten to were spitting and sparking: the sound made Nathan wince as he stepped in through the watertight doors. Commander Ford was off to one side, supervising the replacement of a computer console. As he looked up and registered Nathan's presence, he re-acquired that troubled look which Nathan had noted before. Ford got up from where he had been bent over one of the technicians and came over to Nathan.

'How's she holding up?' Nathan said.

Ford sighed. 'Exterior hull integrity isn't great, but acceptable. The outer pliant skin resealed itself ... as designed.' He glanced at the busy men and women working on the machinery around him. 'The tech equipment in here – we'll do our best. Even at that, we won't have full engines.'

'What you're saying,' Bridger said, 'is that we have four flat tires and a defective spare.'

Wearily, Ford nodded. 'Lieutenant Hitchcock reports eleven other systems have crashed in other parts of the boat so far. Primarily systems having to do with propulsion and weapons.'

Too damn effective ... Nathan thought again. *If this is a malfunction, it's a damned useful one for whoever's gunning for us out there* ... 'Cause?' he said.

Ford shook his head, looking embarrassed. 'Unknown.'

Nathan considered several words that would be satisfying to say, loudly – but there was no telling whether someone's children might wander by outside. 'Anybody checked to see if the warranty's run out on this thing? ...' he said.

Then he let out a long breath. There was no point in dwelling only on the negative side of the situation. 'We've room enough to bring all the survivors from the power station on board,' Bridger said, looking at Ford. 'We should feel good about that.'

Ford didn't look like he felt good about anything: he looked like a man with a mental bellyache, or maybe a moral one. 'What's bothering you, Commander?' Nathan said.

Ford hesitated. 'Captain,' he said, 'about what happened back on the Bridge. I – I shouldn't have –'

Nathan shook his head. 'It's okay. I doubt this situation was covered in the manual.'

'Yes, sir,' Ford said. But the look on his face did not change.

It's got to be dealt with, whatever it is, Bridger thought, despite all his misgivings. *Dammit –* 'Is there something else, Commander?'

Ford looked around him at the frantically-working crew, then said: 'He knew, sir.'

There was only one '*he*' that Nathan could think of at the moment. The same one as always. He began to consider whether losing his temper would serve any useful purpose just now. Probably not, though it would certainly make him feel better.

'Not here,' Bridger said. 'Come on.'

*

The minisub staging area with its moon pool was deserted: it also had the virtue of being big enough to pace in when you were furious. Bridger paced.

'I should have told the truth from the start,' Ford said. 'Orders or not. I knew as well.'

'About this renegade sub,' Nathan said. 'And Noyce knew from the very beginning of this farce.'

'The Admiral figured you'd never come back if you knew the real reason –'

'He's damn right I wouldn't!' Nathan heard the edge of his own anger, suppressed it for the moment. 'How long have you known about the thing?'

'The UEO's known about that sub for almost two months now,' Ford said. 'It's manned by high tech pirates – freebooters. A lot of old subs sold for scrap get grabbed up by guys like this, though until recently most of the trouble has been off Europe. The UEO's tracked this one from up in the Aleutians. She's been making her way along the Seamount Chain – raiding various outposts for supplies, some valuables. But they never took any lives ... until now.'

'Until now.' *Until* we *turned up*, Nathan thought. *Us specifically*. 'So,' he said, 'my "friend" Admiral Noyce sent us off on a shakedown cruise in the general territory where this renegade was reported to be. Knowing there was a chance that we'd run into her.' He leaned against a bulkhead, beginning to feel positively weak with anger: possibly a good thing – he couldn't kill anyone, couldn't even punch anyone's lights out, while he felt this way. *But later –!* This was supposed to be some sort of *easy* example,' Nathan said. 'For me to see how *necessary* I was to this ... *important* cause.'

Ford said nothing at all – which to Nathan was acquiescence enough.

Bridger began to pace again, waving his arms: the scenario was all too clear. 'And if we came across her – you were supposed to hand over command to me. I'd subdue this sitting duck with my super-sub – and bingo, I'm back on the team. ... *Damn* him!'

Ford had the grace to look almost terminally embarrassed. 'Sir,' he said. 'I am not in a position to judge the – merits – of the Admiral's plan. But he could not – *did* not foresee our current circumstances.' He paused. 'Dead in the water: the renegade sub now killing innocent colonists and still at large ...' Ford swallowed, hard. 'Considering your performance on the Bridge during the critical moments of our engagement with the enemy, and taking into account your obvious superior knowledge of this craft – I strongly recommend that you do now take command of this vessel for the duration of this mission.'

Nathan had to stop and take notice of that, for this time Ford clearly wasn't doing it under orders: this time he was saying what he really meant.

But – 'Mission,' Bridger said. 'Now it's a *mission*.' The fury started to boil up, and the urge to tell Ford where to put his command, and come to think of it, *seaQuest* herself. It would be a tight fit, but ... *No.* He calmed himself.

'Let me try to explain something to you,' he said. 'Six years ago I turned my back on all of this. I walked away and I erased this part of my life. I did that for a reason.'

'Your son,' Ford said.

Nathan looked at him, shocked. 'What do you know about my son?'

'I know he was in the Navy,' Ford said. 'That he was killed in action somewhere in the Atlantic.'

The concern on Ford's face brought Nathan up short. 'That's right,' he said after a moment. 'And I promised my wife I'd never have anything to do with the military again. I gave her my word.'

Ford looked at him, his face very still. The troubled expression was all gone: but there was something there now even more difficult to deal with – compassion, but compassion with a hard, cold edge on it. 'With all due respect,' he said, 'there's three hundred men, women and children down at that power station who could care less about your "word" ... *sir.*'

Nathan looked at him, and found that this time, no matter how much he wanted to lose himself in it, the rage would not come up at all.

Trapped, Nathan thought. *Trapped.*

It was no consolation to be trapped in something of his own design, a destiny he himself had literally shaped, on the drawing board, and elsewhere.

But he couldn't run out on it now.

Couldn't? Or wouldn't?

The back of his mind, often so vociferous, now gave him no answer.

Ford was still standing there: waiting, not for anything else to happen, but for his commanding officer to do something, to make his wishes known. Bridger knew the pose. God knew he had held it often enough in his ... career.

'Thank you, Commander,' he said very quietly, dismissing him.

Ford went away.

*

Under the harsh lights, a paper chart lay out on the map table, under glass, with calipers and T-square and the other old-fashioned navigational aids: even, off to one side, a copy of *Haswell's Navigators' Pocket Book* and a slide rule: for while computers might break and calculators might wear their batteries out, a slide rule always worked, and so did a book.

The hand reached down with a grease pencil and marked the third of three possible courses on the glass. Marilyn Stark looked at the results, put down the grease pencil, and sighed: an uncharacteristic sound, from her. Maxwell looked at her uncertainly.

'We're only a few miles away,' he said. 'We can go back and wait for her to come up ...'

Stark shook her head. 'Come up? She never *has to* come up. Even in her crippled state she could stay right down there for *months*.' She pursed her lips. '... No, I'm afraid we have to *draw* her out.'

She reached across the map, tapped one spot with two sets of red-pencilled lines leading to it. 'There. The West

Ridge Undersea Farming Community.' She looked at the map thoughtfully. 'Sounds pleasant, doesn't it? The kind of place I'd like to retire to someday. Someplace I can sit on the porch and tell stories of battles hard fought and *won* to my grandchildren. Like *my* grandfather did with me ...'

She looked off into the shadows of her Bridge. What were they farming, she wondered? The temperature fluctuations in these parts would make kelp an untrustworthy crop, and the farm was much too deep for the littoral crops like carageenan or dulse. No, it would probably be one of the midrange crops, either farmed protein plankton or calciferous yeast, labor-intensive, but high-yielding and bringing a good price on the open market. They probably did a little sediment processing too, scavenging the plentiful manganese nodules from the surrounding ocean floor and maintaining a few small robots to 'pan' for the more valuable nodules of copper, cobalt and nickel. In these parts there might even be the chimney of a 'black smoker', one of those natural hot-water vents where they could collect settled-out iron and manganese and zinc for their own use. It would all be difficult, tedious work, a hard life; but there would be satisfying evenings at the end of it, spent around the warmth of the family hearth. They might even have the satisfaction of burning natural gas from their own little well in those hearthfires –

She looked up from the map and found Maxwell staring at her. *The man looks like he's seen a ghost*, she thought; *what ails him? He used to be able to manage stress so well, but it's the old problem, I suppose: men just lose the ability to cope after a while* ... It was too bad, but she had no time to waste worrying about him. 'What is it?' she said.

He gestured at the map. 'That's nothing but a bunch of homesteaders ...'

Stark stared him down, then smiled a small, cold smile as she marked a cross squarely over the center of the community. 'Exactly,' she said. 'That's the whole point.'

SEVEN

The *seaQuest* lay still and silent, hovering in the dark water over the dimming lights of the power station. Bit by bit, Gedrick Station was seemingly vanishing into the darkness as mechanical and support systems were shut down, or failed, or in some places, the inhabited parts of the station, were simply left and those inhabitants, as carefully as if they were coming back, turned out the lights behind them.

Down among the towers – the few of them that still stood upright, and the ones that were bent and twisted – a small strange device spurted past in the dark, leaving a tiny trail of bubbles behind it. An untrained observer might have thought it was some kind of squid, if a squid could swim without moving its tentacles, if a squid was made of metal, with odd glass and metal protuberances apparently glued onto it here and there. It was not a squid. It had numerous arms, but they were metal, not meat; it had a beak, but one made of sensor-probes rather than bone; it had a brain, but the brain was elsewhere.

The device swam downward, toward the power station, through an eerily clear landscape: one from which all the water seemed to have been removed, so that every physical detail stood up sharp and real, almost too real – a view more like flying than swimming.

On the Bridge of *seaQuest*, Hitchcock sat at her station, being the brain for the distant 'body', seeing the hyperreal view. She was wearing the HyperReality Probe's headset and gloves. They were very new yet, having been installed barely a week before; and they were prototypes – there had been no time to streamline them or cover up the unsightly 'techie' bits, the chips and conduits. Both were simple steel-wire frames with lots of exposed cabling and connectors. Hitchcock's eyes did not need to be covered by the helmet: virtual-reality technology had come along that far, at least, in its last thirty years of development and had bypassed clumsy output methods like screens and retinal projection for the elegance of direct neural contact. Hitchcock had an optic nerve implant laid under the skin of her left temple, ready for such business, and now a single fibre-optic touchplate was pressed gently over the implant, snugged down secure against its pad of neural-conductor foam. The fibre ran from it down to the control console, interfacing with the port-fibres from the gloves.

Hitchcock sat there, her eyes open, observing: but not observing anything in the room – seeing things elsewhere, hearing, feeling, things outside. 'The next best thing to being there,' she said softly.

The probe looked where she looked, moved where she moved. It was easier and safer than sending out a diver – especially at such depths and pressures: few suits and fewer people could handle diving this deep. Now she sent the HR probe zipping among the damaged buildings of the power station. She glanced off to the left: the probe glanced with her, and then up as she looked up. Above her was a bundled tangle of large, ugly pipes. She blinked to change the view, switched to a colorful thermographic view of the same pipes, seeing directly where hot gas ran, where it was cool, and where, in the skins of the pipes themselves, recent friction still lay latent as heat, betraying stress-spots and fractures.

Hitchcock stretched her fingers, considering what the best way was to continue with her investigation. Following her gesture, the probe reconfigured its arms to fit more easily among the pipes.

She sat there a good while more – a muscle-twitch, a slight move, serving to guide the probe through the shattered forest of pipes and conduits. And suddenly, she saw what she had been half-suspecting would be there: what she had been afraid of. 'Uh-oh ...' Then, louder, 'Uh, there's something here – I think you two'd better take a look at it ...'

Nathan had been watching Ford working over his own station: now they stepped over to Hitchcock's, and peered at the screen. Ford looked at Nathan, extremely concerned. 'Wardroom,' he said. 'Let's get everyone we can in there.'

*

The wardroom was standing-room only. Representatives from the military and science sides, by an unconscious choice, Nathan thought, had sorted themselves out onto separate sides of the table. Nathan sat with Ford on one side: Kristin Westphalen stood on the other, looking grim and businesslike. All her attention was for the screen in the middle of the table, showing the HR-probe's thermographic view of the power station's central derrick. Mostly the colors showing there were cool blues and greens, except for a bloom of red-orange heat from the base of it.

Westphalen looked extremely worried. 'As you can see from the data Lieutenant Hitchcock got back from the probe,' she said, 'the power station is built over a deep ocean volcanic vent.'

'Why?' Ford said.

'Energy,' said Nathan. 'It uses trapped heat from the controlled venting to power its turbines.'

'A common enough arrangement,' Westphalen finished for him. 'But according to the data from that probe –' and she pointed at the telltale cloud of orange-red gathering at the base of the derrick – 'the venting cap at the base of the station is in the process of tearing.'

People on the science side stirred and murmured, exchanging concerned glances. Nathan's eyes got a bit wide.

'What happens if it breaks?' Hitchcock said.

Westphalen shook her head. 'A nightmare. If it tears completely, the poisonous extract gases that are usually captured and disposed of will spill out across the ocean floor.'

'How big a spread?' asked Ford.

Westphalen shook her head, looking concerned with the enormity of what the data had told her. 'With the thermal currents in this territory – could be *hundreds* of miles.'

The science team all began to talk at once, angry, upset, and worried by turns. Westphalen raised her voice enough to be heard over the din. 'Every living undersea biologic – plant and animal – would choke on this manmade crap and *die!*' She looked at the naval personnel across the table, a pleading expression. 'We'd have our first equivalent of a deep ocean desert wasteland!'

The noise among the science crew got louder. To Nathan's annoyance, the naval crew were mostly sitting looking at each other with expressions going from blank unconcern to annoyance that such fuss was being made about so little. He spoke to Westphalen through the commotion, but she couldn't hear him, shook her head, cupped one hand behind her ear. Nathan raised his voice, imitating that DI shout he had heard his own officers copy so often in his younger day. *'Can it be fixed?'*

Stunned by Bridger's sheer unexpected volume, everyone shut up. Westphalen looked at him in something like astonishment, and Nathan realized with some surprise that she had not expected him to be on her side. 'Yes,' she said. 'Given the proper equipment.'

Ford frowned a bit. 'You mean *military* equipment.'

Bridger shook his head in genial disgust. *How am I going to get through to these people that if the paradigm doesn't work on this level, it won't work on any other?* 'I don't care *who* owns the pink slip!'

He watched Ford. You could almost see the wheels go around in the man's head as he tried to make the right decision. His naval personnel were all staring at him, though, expecting him to jump the obvious way, *their* way: and there was no way this officer, youngest Ex-O or not, no matter how little experience he might have had, could not feel the pressure and be urged to jump that way. Indeed, he wanted to anyhow. 'I understand the Doctor's concern, but ...'

Oy, Bridger thought, wanting to roll his eyes as he heard

the too-clear emphasis on the word 'Doctor'. *He* is *going to put his foot in it – as far as he can!* 'This ship is operating under very unusual and dangerous circumstances,' Ford went on. 'And presently, I don't know if we should divert our efforts from the very real need to find the cause of weapons and propulsion systems failure – so we can go after that armed rebel sub out there.'

'Commander,' Nathan said, 'in my own days among my military brethren, I would've taken the same stance you're taking now. However ...' – and he held up his hand to forestall the look of satisfaction that was going back and forth among the naval types – 'if I understand this whole UEO mandate thing correctly, then this ship shouldn't sail away from a potential major ecological disaster *if* it can do something about it.' The science personnel blinked at that. 'I know I'm only along for the ride here,' Nathan said, all innocence. 'But only so many TeamCraft and EVA suits can work on our hull at any given time, so –' and he looked sidewise at Ford most pointedly – 'I *strongly* recommend we patch that vent.'

Ford paused, saying nothing: studying his hands. He looked torn. But Bridger simply waited, not needing to say anything else. This man might be young and moderately inexperienced as yet, but clearly he knew when something was right. Finally, he looked up and nodded. 'All right, Captain Bridger. We patch the vent.'

Some of the naval personnel breathed out in muffled exasperation. 'Dismissed,' Ford said, and science and military staff alike started to head out.

Nathan looked over at Westphalen as he got up. She was plainly extremely pleased, but her own management style wasn't going to let her show how much: certainly not in front of these Navy types, and maybe not in front of her own people.

He went over to her. 'Can I buy you a cup of coffee?' he said.

She glanced at him, a quizzical look, then nodded.

*

In the officers' lounge, they sat down with their cups and spent a short time in the cream-and-sugar ritual. There was a monitor nearby, and Nathan activated it and had a look at the Docking Bay area. In the pale glare of the auxiliary lighting, the place was turning into the scene of a mêlée. Off to one side, the Docking Bay Control Officer stood at his station, monitoring the deployment of the several TeamCraft on his display screens. Below him, streaming toward the docking port, a cluster of science crew came carrying their equipment – various monitors, chemical analyzers, and so forth – mixing uncomfortably with a group of military crew carrying their own gear. Both teams were waiting to go up the ladders to the waiting TeamCraft, but there was no mixing, no chatter between them, no friendly banter. Instead, there were glares.

Visible on the display screens at the control officer's station, several TeamCraft, each with its two-person crew, were already on their way toward the smoking base of the power station derrick. One vanished into the smoke while the Control Officer watched. Others were still in the process of pushing away from the *seaQuest*'s Docking Sphere section.

Westphalen was looking over his shoulder as he switched views to what one of the TeamCraft was seeing, the swirls of toxic vapor from around the base of the power station. She breathed out, looked over at Bridger and said, 'Thank you for what you did back there.'

Nathan shrugged as he turned away from the monitor. 'It made sense.'

She looked at him curiously. 'Excuse me for saying so – but you don't strike me as the prototypical military man.'

He was intrigued in spite of himself. 'Really? Exactly how do I "strike" you, Doctor?'

Westphalen looked embarrassed. 'Now I've insulted you.'

Bridger laughed softly. 'On the contrary. I've spent most of my career trying not to become part of the machine.'

'Then you consider yourself a radical?'

He raised his eyebrows. 'I never thought about it one way or the other. I made up my mind a long time ago that I wouldn't "go along" to "get along".' He thought of Carol, then, remembering how she would tease him about what she called his 'troublemaking' – 'My wife used to call me "terminally stubborn",' he said.

Westphalen hesitated a moment. 'She must have seen a glint of flexibility?'

Nathan smiled slightly and stirred his coffee again. 'Perhaps a glint.'

'How long were you married?'

'Twenty-seven years. She died ten months ago.'

'I'm sorry,' Westphalen said; and even while busily blocking the resurgence of the memories that inevitably came with the words 'She died –', Nathan could tell from Westphalen's tone that the question wasn't mere idle curiosity.

'What about you?' he said. 'Is there a Mr Westphalen?'

'Several, I'm afraid.'

Bridger raised his eyebrows again. 'Interesting.'

But Westphalen was shaking her head. 'Not really. I can't even tell you what went wrong, specifically. I guess in the end they were just – weak. Strength can be a debilitating trait for some men.' She sighed. 'I did get one positive thing out of it.'

'Alimony?' Nathan said innocently.

She gave him a look not nearly as annoyed as she should have. 'My daughter, Susan. She just received her degree in biophysics. I hope to have her join my research team. – Do you have children?'

That set of memories started to come up, too, and Nathan pushed them down forcefully. 'We had a son,' he said. 'He was lost at sea six years ago.'

Westphalen looked at him, clearly unable to find exactly what to say, so she retreated back into cooler mode. 'You wanted to talk to me about something?'

He was glad enough to retreat himself. 'Uh, yeah. – I need a troubleshooter.'

'A what?'

'I don't think what's happening to this boat is an accident. I need somebody who can tear her systems apart and find out what's going on.'

'What about Lieutenant Hitchcock?'

'No good,' Nathan said. 'She's hardware. Besides, she's busy supervising the repair team. I need somebody who can get into her guts and dig around. I was hoping you might have somebody on your team?'

'I –' She looked doubtful: Nathan started to worry. Then she blinked. 'Wait. There *is* one person who might be able to help.'

'Who?' Nathan said, getting up. 'Let's go see them –'

*

They came around the corner of a quarters entryway, where light played on a wall. Nathan looked at the wall, opened his mouth, and shut it again. Someone was making giant shadow bunnies on it.

He and Westphalen stuck their heads around the next corner, the room's actual doorway. The auxiliary lights were too pale to produce the result they were seeing; a battery-powered lamp had been rigged near the room's bunk. On the bunk itself, hands up in front of the light, lay a boy, making the handshadows. It was Lucas.

Lucas glanced up in some surprise, with a single movement of his hands turned the bunny into a dog face and said, with the 'dog's' jaws moving in time, 'Wowee, Lucas! Look who's come to visit us today! It's the Amazing Bonko and his beautiful assistant Doris!'

Nathan looked at Westphalen, his eyebrows so far up they probably looked like they were planning to emigrate to his scalp. 'You're serious?' he said.

Westphalen nodded. 'Some things,' she said, 'are worth putting up with.'

'I'll believe it when I see it,' Nathan said.

Within a few minutes, though, the lamp had been swiveled down to do what it had originally been intended to do: illuminate Lucas's workstation. Nathan found himself becoming impressed despite himself. The workstation was filled with every kind of computer component he could imagine – keyboards, memoryboards, wiring everywhere, jury-rigged serial and parallel ports, CD-ROM and block

ROM and components he couldn't identify – all inter-mingled with the usual clutter and junk you might expect in a fourteen-year-old's room: socks in pairs and mismatched triplets, underwear – one set of it being worn upside down over a teddybear's head – clothing in various states of repair and cleanliness draped over everything, here and there used as insulation matting or cushions to keep one wire-entangled piece of electronic equipment from touching another; and some of them plainly just thrown on the floor because their owner had no time for them.

Lucas was hunched over the workstation, hammering at it – not so much in the style of a classical pianist, more like a jazz drummer, all the action coming from the wrists, going from snares to cymbals to brushes to cowbells and back to the snares again – occasionally reaching out to another keyboard nearby to hit a control key here, tap in a sequence there, bring up a macro from somewhere else. All this would have looked very impressive, had Lucas not at the time been wearing a baseball cap with a dolphin snout out the front and its tail out the back. He was muttering to himself, but the language was so interspersed with computer and other jargon Nathan couldn't translate that he realized there was no point in him standing there trying to understand what was going on: *just let the boy take his course*, Nathan thought, and left him to the business of working his way into the ship's systems.

He wandered over to the bookshelves. There were a lot of them, bracketed to the walls. Some of them actually held books, but these were much in the minority. Most of them were covered with ... *stuff*. There was one of the little laser-disc players that Nathan remembered from his own youth, the ones that had been so much fun to listen to on planes until they discovered that the things interfered with the on-board electronics, and an even older tape-cassette machine – though looking at this one now, he couldn't imagine what had been so great about a tape-deck that couldn't record. And thinking of recordings ... Nathan reached out and picked up what had to be a computer disk, one of the big old fragile floppies that left a good slice of the recording medium exposed to any dust or sticky fingers that might wander by. Other things: a cap with a big X on it, some kind of stuffed saurian raptor. 'What's all this?' he muttered.

Lucas actually got up and, very gently, took the floppy disk away from him, leaning it back on the shelf, on edge. 'My collection,' he said, suddenly sounding astonishingly protective. 'Antiques. Everything up there's from the 1990s.'

Nathan looked at the odd conglomeration of stuff. *Antiques,* he thought. *I had some of this stuff and I thought they were pretty neat. Now they're antiques. What does that make me?*

'Why the '90s?' Westphalen said.

Lucas shrugged. 'Because it's all so – old-fashioned, and weird ...'

Old-fashioned and weird. Right. Nathan wasn't sure he wouldn't prefer to be an antique after all. At least there was a certain amount of dignity in the word. He picked up another baseball cap, this one with brown stains on it which suggested that someone had gotten playful with their ice cream. UNIVERSAL TOURS, it said. Nathan shook his head, put it down again.

Lucas was still working furiously. He paused a moment, waiting, watching the screen – then went taut. 'Got it!' he said.

Bridger looked at the screen and wondered exactly what he had got, unless it was one of the more abstruse entertainment channels. The monitor was displaying an arcane mixture of colors, geometrics, data scrolling behind some things that might have been part of a flow chart, except that flow chart fields had never come in shapes like *those*, as far as Nathan knew. He couldn't make head or tail of it: he was glad Lucas could.

The boy tapped at the keyboard, bringing up new screenfuls of data, new flowcharts and diagrams, more scrolling text. 'You were right,' he said over his shoulder to Nathan, sat back from the screen, and waved at it. Whatever sense he made of the graphics was lost on Nathan, but he wasn't about to say so. Instead he just raised his eyebrows a notch and waited for an explanation. As he had guessed, it wasn't long in coming – though as computer-experts' explanations went, it was short enough. And not encouraging. 'There's the source of your trouble. The main computer's dying.'

'*Dying?*'

Lucas spun his chair slowly around. 'The core of the main computer has a virus. That's what's gnawing away at the systems ...'

'If it's in the core,' Westphalen said, 'why isn't it affecting the whole ship?'

'Oh, it will,' Lucas said. 'It just started with weapons and propulsion.'

'But why didn't the system diagnostics catch it on routine checks?'

'No,' Nathan said. 'When weapons and propulsions go down, the system only runs a *quick-pass* diagnostics program – conventional wisdom being either you find and fix such a problem fast – or you're dead anyway. Unless you fixed that too ...?'

'I've got some parts on order,' Lucas said right back, unperturbed. Nathan gave him an old-fashioned look entirely appropriate to an antique, and watched it bounce off the boy's shell of cheeky self-assurance.

Westphalen straightened up from staring at the screen. Evidently what she saw there made a good deal more sense than it did to Bridger, because she had the look of someone who didn't like what they were looking at. 'I still don't see how it could have been missed.'

Lucas nodded, bringing up another screenful of data. 'The complication here was that this sucker's buried so deep that any quick-pass sweep couldn't find it.' He looked impressed. 'It's pretty cool. I mean, whoever planted this thing really knew what they were doing.'

'Then it's not organic,' Nathan said.

'No way. It's too specific.'

Nathan leaned over his shoulder, looking at the screenful of incomprehensibles. *I knew that something was amiss,* he thought. *We've come a long way from the time when the only form of sabotage was to throw a wooden shoe into the works … Who would purposely leave such a mine in our midst … something scheduled to fail our systems, maybe kill us, at the time when we needed it the most?* He put that aside. 'Can you tell how long it's been in there?'

Lucas looked smug – or anyway, more smug than usual. 'No problem,' he said. 'If I can peel back the layers of data between me and it –' He began hammering on the keyboards again.

Nathan smiled. There might after all be some purpose for the arrogance of youth. Anyway, if he produced the results … who really cared?

'It's a little tricky,' Lucas said as he worked, sounding

very pleased with himself at having a chance to lecture his elders. 'They don't usually hang date tags on these things. It's not a file – it's a fragment of code and even if it had any dating attached to it, that could have been erased, subverted, told to lie ... No, you have to analyze these things structurally. Judging by the layers of data accreted between the upper levels of processing and the virus, it might have been hiding in there for as long as a year. Dormant ... just waiting until someone started to use those systems. And use them in *action*, not in a drill.'

'Systems that would only be used when the ship went into battle,' Bridger muttered.

Then, 'Whoa!' Lucas yelped, pulled his hands up off the keys as if they'd been singed and pushed himself and his chair back away from the grouped keyboards.

Westphalen stared at him. 'What?'

'What's wrong?' Nathan half-expected to see smoke, or sparks, or something obvious to have provoked a reaction like that.

'It's got dogs,' Lucas said, frowning at the screen. Nathan shook his head, very briefly wondering whether that little poodle had gotten into the computer core somehow.

'Watchdogs,' Lucas said, with exaggerated clarity, as if explaining matters to three-year-olds. 'Sub-programs set up to protect the virus. If I mess with any of them, the whole ship could crash and burn. Life support, the works ...'

He looked at their expressions and matched them for shakenness. 'You heard the old saying, "let sleeping dogs lie" ...?' Lucas shook his head, folded his arms and glared at the screen.

Bridger stood there, absorbing it. The fury was building in him now, at someone who could so successfully make the weapon in his hand, the ship that he had designed, into a useless thing, a lump, a liability. But he was not going to let it stop him. It was possible that there was something in this equation that whoever had committed this sabotage had not reckoned with. He would find it. He would use it.

He would make them *sorry.*

'Captain to the Bridge,' said a loudspeaker nearby. 'Captain to the Bridge –'

'I think that's you,' Lucas said.

Nathan nodded, already heading out. 'Do the best you can,' he said, then halfway to the door he paused, and looked back. 'Hey, kid –'

Lucas raised his eyebrows at him.

'Good job,' Nathan said, and went out, but not before seeing – with some satisfaction – the shadow of a smile of surprise starting to form on Lucas's face.

*

He left Lucas's quarters and started making his way back up to the Bridge, pushing his anger down to the point where it would not run him, but merely be a useful tool, something he could use to keep himself going.

His mood did not improve … there was nothing that could be done about that. He wanted to find the saboteur and wring his, her or their necks, in order if need be, until his hands were sore.

Meanwhile, he slipped back into the place where he was most likely to be of use. Ford met him as he came in. 'We're picking up a satlink video transmission,' he said. 'Distress call –'

'From where?'

'A small farming outpost.'

'I've got a partial signal now,' O'Neill called.

Nathan turned. 'Put it on the main screen –'

The screen came to life and showed a very weak television signal, badly cluttered with depth artifact and distortion. It kept drifting out. The only thing that could be made out on it with any certainty was the vague shape of a man, bending with the distortion, then righting itself again. It was someone broadcasting unboosted from some distance away under sea.

Sound was clear enough: sound was always the first thing to come in and the last to be lost on a given carrier. And there were sounds of agitation, pandemonium, going on behind the man: he kept turning from side to side, looking behind him, reacting to the trouble. '... aymond Brenner,' his voice said weakly, wiped out then by a blast of static, then coming out strongly again. '... am Territorial Governor ... West Ridge Farm ... Community ...!'

O'Neill was fiddling with his controls, trying to get a better signal. It snapped in again in a hail of static. '... been attacked without provocation,' said the desperate voice, 'by a renegade craft!'

The whole image jittered as something exploded behind him, rocking the camera mount, the floor, the walls, everything else. The man managed to keep his feet, but only just. '– Why are they doing this? –' Another blast of heavy static cut across what he was saying. '... any ship within the sound of my voice ... *please help us*!'

The image danced and jumped. A voice was heard behind him in a moment of horrible clarity when the static died right away. 'The canopy is giving way!!'

The Territorial Governor turned back toward the camera. 'Please!' he cried. 'Someone help us! Some –'

– and it was gone: only faint snow and feedback sparkles remained on the screen, depth artifact and nothing else.

There had been murmurs on the Bridge until now, people reacting to what they were hearing. Now everyone fell silent. One crewwoman said low, to the crewman beside her, 'We could've helped them if we weren't wasting our time patching that stupid vent to protect a few fish.'

Bridger overheard the remark. He suspected he had been meant to. At the moment, with all those eyes on him, he found it difficult to disagree.

'Should I recall the repair team and set course?' Ford said quietly to Nathan.

'No', Nathan said.

'But –'

'You've got a job to do right here,' Nathan said. 'When you've finished locating the rest of the people at the power station, then we can deal with it.'

Ford nodded.

'I'll be in my quarters,' Nathan said. 'I'd appreciate it if you'd keep me updated on the repair efforts?'

'Yes, sir.'

Nathan looked at the dark forward screen, met the mass gaze of the Bridge crew without blinking – then straightened himself and headed out.

*

He shut his door, leaned against it for a moment. Only here could he let himself feel the full weight of what he had seen on the Bridge: the anguish, the horror, the helplessness.

Death. There was a time, had been many times, when he had looked it in the face and stood his ground. Never unmoved – it would be a dangerous officer, in his opinion, who could do that: someone who would be too incautious with other people's lives. But he had coped with it, nonetheless.

He had even coped when Eric had died. He still remembered looking up from his work to see Bill Noyce standing in the doorway of his old office, looking stricken. Everybody at that point had heard about the trouble going on in the Arctic, the tension between the North Pacific forces and the Aleutian Group; when the shooting started, the scuttlebutt had gone around the offices like lightning, but there had been very few details. Nathan had ignored the gossip and the noise and had concentrated on his work. Not until he looked up and saw Bill standing there did it come home to him that something had happened, and not just to someone else: to *him*.

His son with the infectious laugh, the intense desire for knowledge, the utter certainty that he was invulnerable: dead, and for nothing. It hadn't even been a proper battle – as if that would have helped – just a dirty little clash between two ships whose commanders both had itchy trigger-fingers and not enough courage to back down. Nathan had coped even then, through the horror of having to go home and tell Carol, the dreadfulness of identifying the body, the ravaging funeral which had to be conducted with dignity, for the sake of the others who grieved as much as in Eric's honor.

He remembered the nights he had held Carol and cried:

both while he was still trying to work out how to deal with the terrible thing that had happened to them, and after he had made up his mind what to do about it – after he had resigned from the Navy, and moved himself and Carol away from the wars and rumors of wars, to the quiet of the deserted island off the Yucatan. It was only Carol, he realized now, who had made it possible for him to cope during that awful time: only her silent support, only her courage.

For now she was gone too, and the root of his ability to cope was gone.

Death.

He had been a military man, used to the idea that you might die in the service of something bigger than yourself. His long familiarity with that concept, and knowing his son was familiar with it too, was one of the things that had helped to keep him in one piece through the grief of Eric's loss. But it was another matter to die of something useless, something you were helpless against, something that came and took you, irrationally, by stealth, in the night – the way it had taken Carol.

One evening it had seemed simply as if she had caught cold. Carol had made light of it, had gone to bed early that night and had told Nathan she would lie out in the sun next day and 'bake it out of her'. But the next morning other forces than the sun were baking her: the fever had taken hold and was burning away her slender body like a stick in a fire. Her temperature was already nearly a hundred and four when Nathan woke beside her to find her tossing and moaning in the grip of delirium. He had no idea what had caused so sudden an illness, and in great fear had done what he swore he would never do again – turned on the radiolink and called the mainland for help. Then he had set about trying to bring Carol's temperature down with brine packs. But it was already too late, and by the time help arrived two hours later, she was gone ...

The diagnosis of a rare tropical disease had only infuriated and grieved him, more than her death itself. He had given her to the sea, and resolved to have nothing further to do with the world which was so much faster at delivering death than a chance for life. He had turned his back steadfastly on death, determined at best, with his research, to fight it, at least, to ignore it. Now, though, he found how futile the attempt had been. Those helpless screams echoed in his head, cousins to Carol's dying moans, and to Eric's cries that Nathan had heard in nightmare for so long, despite never having heard them in life. Hearing the desperate cries from the farming community, it was as if Carol and Eric had died all over again, and wounds that Nathan had foolishly thought healed, or at least sealed over, were open again, and throbbing.

He shook his head and let out a long breath, then touched the pad to bring up the lights and looked around. His cabin – not as small as some he had had, not as big as others, but comfortable enough: bed, desk bay with desk and computer, a sea-window nearby, the view out of it dark except for the occasional bloom of light from a passing TeamCraft, and off to one side, the door to the head. His bags were on the bed and an envelope lay there beside them.

He went to the bed, picked up the envelope with his name on it, opened the note inside it, read it.

Swallowed. Nathan glanced over at the desk bay, twitching slightly.

They did it, then. Somehow.

I refuse to be afraid of this —

— but, irrationally, he was.

Nonetheless, he walked slowly over to the desk bay. He stood over the desk for a moment, then slid the keyboard out of the console and looked it over. Nathan glanced at the piece of paper in his hand, entered the password written on it on the keyboard and waited, his heart hammering.

The light in the room went dark and moody. *Now is that the computer*, he thought, turning, *or a grayout* —

He turned.

— and blinked, and stared, because in the middle of the now dimmer room, a swirl of light was beginning to form.

A human shape began to structure itself from that light. From the abnormal clarity and brilliance of the colors, Nathan could see now that it was a hologram forming, the details steadying down now: a man, a little stooped, a little stocky, in tweed jacket and twills, white-haired. The face resolved itself into an image as sharp as any photograph's: a lined face, much lived in, very old, but very sharp and wise, and essentially kind.

The old man stood there and looked at him.

'Professor Danielson?' Nathan said.

'Hello, Nathan ...' the old man said. 'Welcome back.'

EIGHT

Gedrick Station was a mess. For all the work that had gone on, and was still going on, the *seaQuest* engineers might as well have saved their time for tasks aboard the submarine. Its primary derrick and exchanger-stack were still wreathed in the filthy clouds of pollutant waste that came smoking from the ruptured vent. Swirls of heat-distorted water mingled with the foulness, sending it spiralling like drunken sea-snakes through the jumble of smashed structural bracing that was the legacy of the *Delta*'s attack.

The patching operation wasn't just hot, sweaty, dirty work; it was dangerous, too. Every now and then something shifted deep within the tangle, and a couple of tons of jagged ironwork moved together with a sound like the crunch of massive metallic jaws. *seaQuest*'s EVA suits were armoured, and the TeamCraft were proofed against most of the hazards of pressure – but against what could happen here, they were no sturdier than blown eggshells. Every time the wreckage settled, they had to move clear or risk the consequences, and that meant whatever task was only half-completed remained that way until it was safe to move back into the area. Only the unmanned welding-crabs specifically designed for hazardous deep-sea operation were able to stay in place; and though they could be crushed without loss of life, *seaQuest*'s engineering team had only so many of the little automatons to spare. They were already looking nervously at the inventory listings, because one more drawback about putting to sea for nothing more than a twenty-four hour shakedown cruise meant that those inventories showed nothing like full.

*

Nathan Bridger knew nothing of Engineering Section's difficulties. He had enough problems of his own. Every time he thought that he was coming to terms with *seaQuest* and all the things that had been done to 'improve' her since he left the project, some other problem turned up to be dealt with. The appearance of a man he recognized – and knew to be dead – for one thing. Bridger didn't believe in ghosts; he had too much of a rational, sensible, scientific mind for that, and this was only a hologram after all. But when that same rational, sensible mind was confronted with visual evidence, such as a hologram that had taken on the form of his old Academy professor, then it might well be time for a rethink.

'So they've done this too,' Nathan said softly.

He walked slowly around the image: it glanced around to follow him, but otherwise stood still and waited. Nathan reached out thoughtfully to the hologram, staring at the back of his hand to see how the projection would alter. It didn't, even when the hand went right through the tweed jacket and came out on the other side. 'You look even better than I remember from the Academy,' he said. 'But wait a second ... the Navy was refusing to install you. *Had* refused. How'd you get here?'

'Our young Mr Wolenczak,' said the image of Old Man Danielson. 'He brought me online several weeks ago – found the disabled installation routines in the core and enabled them, despite the password locks.' 'He' smiled. 'He's really quite remarkable.'

'So I've noticed.' Nathan came around in front of the image again. It still came as a shock to discover that this particular brainchild of his had grown up without so much as a nod of acknowledgement towards its original parent. But that was unjust. For the past few years, the original parent – Nathan's mind still flinched from all but the most abstract implications of that word – had been as far out of touch as he could get, and if he hadn't been kept up to date on developments, he knew who could take the blame –

'What is your mission?' he said, testing.

'I am a synthetic intelligence, intended to provide a sounding board in times of moral or ethical conflict,' the Old Man said, 'conjoined to a holographic interface for maximum effectiveness of use.'

'Very good,' Nathan said.

The image looked at him with exactly the same wry expression that the real Danielson would have used on any cadet bold enough to tell *him* he had done something right. 'Lucas has given me a wide range of source material to draw on,' the Old Man said. 'In addition, you can change my image by inserting a photograph in the imaging port of the main computer unit.'

'Well, seems like our little friend thought of everything,' Nathan said. 'But why is *this* one the primary image? The

default, as I remember, was supposed to be nonspecific –
a computer-generated officer of equal rank.'

'When Admiral Noyce briefly reactivated the development program a year ago, this was the image and personality
he specified for the demos for the brass.'

'Maximum effectiveness,' Bridger muttered, and paced
around the projection again. He was both amused and
irritated when it began to pace too, keeping in step with
him. *Just for me*, he thought. Noyce was *so* sure that the kid
would come back to the candy-store – and once there, he
would find their old instructor waiting for him, in the not-
very-solid flesh –

The hologram nodded agreement again, and Nathan
knew he would find more comfort in a mechanical awk-
wardness than in this too-smooth, too-human motion. Too
perfect ... 'Someone the Captain can talk to ... when he
can't talk to anyone else,' said 'Danielson's' voice. No,
blast it. Danielson's. Some parts of virtual-reality could be
too real for comfort. 'Someone he can *confide* in. Voice his
innermost questions ... his doubts ...'

Bridger swung around to glare at the hologram. Never
mind his innermost doubts, the thing seemed able to read
his innermost *thoughts*, and formulate a reasoned response
to them.

Unless ...

He hadn't been hiding what he had been thinking, the
way he would have done with a real person. Not that he
was secretive by nature, but there were some things that
were nobody else's business. Was it possible that the
holographic receptors were able to react and counteract to
visual stimuli even more subtle than a change of expression?
He hesitated, wondering just how analytical the circuitry

could be. Knowing the difference between right and wrong had long been a yardstick in courts of law for judging awareness of the potential for guilt or innocence; and the shades of gray that lay to either side of those absolutes made a morass in which psychology researchers could be heard plunging about even today. But a machine ...

'What's *seaQuest*'s current depth?' Nathan said.

'Twenty-two hundred feet.'

'What's the meaning of life?'

'Be more specific,' the Old Man said, exactly as severely as he would have to a cadet who hadn't been exact enough.

'Forget it,' Nathan said, and walked around for a few seconds more. 'Are you familiar with the ship's mainframe?'

The Old Man smiled. 'Nathan, I *am* the mainframe.'

'Right. Then you can track down the virus that's affected the ship?'

'Could you locate the viruses in your own body from your symptoms when you have a cold?' the Old Man said mildly. 'Or locate a growing brain tumor? Sorry, Nathan. My capacities are limited to the data that's fed into my memory units.'

'Great,' Nathan said, pacing.

'This information upsets you?'

'If you're a computer, how can you tell if I'm upset?'

'Your vocal patterns are in considerable deviation from the norm,' the Old Man said. 'Body kinetics are indicative of stress and frustration. Also, your respiration rate is –'

'Never mind,' Nathan said. 'Another option courtesy of Lucas, I suppose –'

The Old Man nodded. Then he said, 'Has your family come aboard with you?'

Nathan stopped in his tracks. Very softly he said, 'Your

data banks are a little behind. Carol and Eric are – they died.'

'I see,' the Old Man said, and the voice was as compassionate as could have been desired. 'Is that why you left the service before finishing *seaQuest*?'

'Yes. I moved to an island. I thought I'd be safe there. I knew that, coming back here, I'd have to ... let people in again.'

'And risk losing them,' the Old Man said.

'Yes.'

'You must have missed your work.'

Nathan shook his head. 'I still had work. Plenty to do. What I really missed was *this*. The sea. I'd forgotten how it felt. My pulse slows down, my head is clear ...' He stopped. 'Why am I telling you all this?'

'Because I'm listening?' the Old Man said. 'Or simply because this is what I'm for, and it's working.'

Nathan laughed at that, and moved to the window looking out into the dark ocean. He put his hands up against the cool glass, feeling, trying to feel the water just on the other side of it. From the dark glass, his face looked back at him.

'There wasn't a day that I didn't think about this,' he said softly, 'no matter what I told myself. Why couldn't I let it go?'

'Because it's a part of you,' the Old Man said. 'It's the best part.'

Slowly Nathan turned to look at the image of the man in his tweeds. 'I'm really glad you're here,' he said.

'Why is that?'

'Because so far on this trip, you're the only one who's told me the truth,' Nathan said.

The Old Man smiled.

*

A heavy clank rang through the docking bay, and the tell-tales to either side of the access hatch glowed bright green in the dimness of the auxiliary lighting aboard *seaQuest*. There was a brief hissing of high-pressure air before the hatch swung open – and water came through it in a solid column, crashing in white foam over the emergency team waiting below.

There was too much water, far too much. Flattened against the farther bulkhead and out of the MedTeam's way, Kristin Westphalen stared anxiously upward. She knew well enough that some overflow was normal even after a hard seal had been established, but never anything like this. It had to come from somewhere, and the only place was from inside the TeamCraft that had just docked. Two of the medics went scrambling up the ladder and came back down again carrying a man in a beige Science Team jumpsuit.

Westphalen stared, recognizing the man, then hurried forward. Of all the people to be involved in Search and Rescue, or Repair and Maintenance, or whatever they had been doing out there, Tim Conway was the least likely. He was puny enough in the lab that was his natural habitat, but here, outweighed by all the brutal bulk of heavy machinery, he looked fragile enough to shatter. Drenched and barely conscious, his head hung loosely back on his shoulders as the MedTeam personnel laid him gently on a stretcher and began stabilization procedures.

Overhead another jumpsuited figure eased out of the

flooded TeamCraft and on board the relative security of *seaQuest*. This suit was black, and it contained Lieutenant Hitchcock. She looked almost as bad as Conway; just as wet, just as shaky, but at least able to move without help. She paused, making sure that her fellow-passenger was in as good shape as could be expected, then came down the ladder very slowly, one rung at a time.

Bridger came into the docking bay at a half-run, slowed down hastily to avoid a collision, and scanned the area. He shortly found himself being scanned, acutely, as well: everyone in the place was staring at him. And at what he was wearing. His uniform. *The* uniform ...

Nathan frowned, hoping he didn't have another shaving cut besides the two he had already patched up. This was only his second shave since leaving the island, and he'd gotten out of the habit. His chin felt naked – and *he* felt naked, despite the fact that the military-black jumpsuit which had been in one of the bags covered much more of him than his original clothes had done.

'What's wrong?' he said, going over to Hitchcock, who was swallowing hot coffee as if there was likely to be a run on supplies. 'You people never seen a uniform before?'

She looked up at him as if she hadn't. 'What happened?' Nathan asked. It wasn't such a pointless question as it seemed. Flooding, for sure. He could see that much already. Though most of the water had drained away by now, the residual splashprint across the deck was enormous. Far too big for the few gallons caught in a TeamCraft's docking collar. The real question wasn't so much 'what?', as 'how?'

Hitchcock shook her head: 'Our aft pressure seals blistered,' she said. 'We started taking on water fast, and I had to rig a temporary patch.'

She gave Bridger a rueful smile, because that was obvious enough already, and glanced past the approaching Doctor Westphalen at the skinny beige-clad figure on the stretcher. The medics had an oxygen mask over his face, but his chest was rising and falling steadily and the readouts were showing a heart-rate that was standard enough, if a bit rapid. In the circumstances, that was hardly surprising.

'We were at a crucial point in the patching procedure. He didn't want to let go until we got it done.' She shook her head. 'I gotta admire the little fella. I could tell he was scared to death, but he stuck it out ...'

'So did *you* ...' Westphalen sounded just as admiring, if reluctant to show it.

'Hey.' Hitchcock looked at her, then at them both, shrugged, and drank more of her salty coffee. 'Gotta save the little fishies ...'

Nathan took note; however casually she tossed the line off, she meant it. This might be the first step towards getting the two halves of his – no, dammit! – of *this* crew working together. He just hoped that it wouldn't need any more near-fatal incidents. What was it they said? Once is an accident, twice is coincidence, and three times is enemy action. Great. They'd had the accident already, and the enemy action was out there somewhere, blowing helpless victims to blazes while *seaQuest* sat here, helpless and unarmed. So where was the coincidence ...?

'What about the hull?' Nathan said.

Hitchcock pitched the paper coffee cup away from her. 'It's not leaking, but it's temporary. We won't be able to fix it right until we get back to Pearl.'

Nathan nodded. 'How much longer are my people gonna have to be out there?' he asked.

Hitchcock looked at him in astonishment. 'Your people...?'

Nathan glared at her, having no time for this. 'Lieutenant – ?'

'Two hours, sir,' Hitchcock said.

He looked around him at the busy medics, and beyond them, beyond *seaQuest*'s hull, out to where the rogue *Delta* was doing ... what? 'I'm not letting anybody die *anywhere* again if I can help it.' He swung back to Hitchcock, and the look on his face was that of a man who had run out of excuses, from himself or anybody else. 'You've got *one* hour. Then we're pulling everybody back and going after that renegade sub.'

He turned at the sound of footsteps. Lucas had come in. 'You find anything?' Nathan said.

'I'm still trying to get at the virus,' Lucas said. 'It's real well-guarded. But I was able to nail the time of entry.'

'And?' Nathan said.

'Based on the data accretion above it, I'd say it was planted thirteen months ago.'

Nathan thought about that for a moment, then nodded and headed out. Behind him, he heard Lucas say softly to Hitchcock, and with some bemusement, 'Did he look different to you?'

Nathan smiled.

*

At almost fourteen thousand tons submerged displacement and near enough five hundred and fifty feet in length, the Type IV *Delta* was one of the largest submarines ever built.

She was surpassed only by the US Navy's *Ohio*-class SSBNs and the huge *Typhoon* PLARBs that had been Fleet-Admiral Chernavin's last and mightiest children.

Then came *seaQuest*.

The *Delta-IV* had met her match at last, and she didn't like it. Though it was only the sound of her own engines driving the gleaming pair of phosphor-bronze screws, it seemed as though the huge boat grumbled softly to herself as she slid through the deep dark. A great white shark swung warily to one side and watched the submarine go by with blank black eyes as big as a man's fist, giving way not from fear – the tiny brain in its huge fanged head didn't know such an emotion – but from respect for something more deadly than itself. The shark was right; but not about the sub.

Marilyn Stark sat at the small desk tucked into her cramped quarters and stared at the faces in a photograph, lost in thoughts of long ago and far away. She could remember the day the shot was taken, and the photographer bustling around the Bridge with his archaic, expensive roll-film camera, clicking away as he arranged and rearranged people until he was satisfied. If she had bothered to recognize anything as useless as happiness now, she would have called those happier days. And a better boat. Her boat. *seaQuest*, not this ex-Soviet antique.

The *Delta* was a capable enough weapon, but it lacked sophistication. It was a cudgel. But *seaQuest* had been a rapier. And what had they done, the UEO Powers that Be? They had taken the rapier from the hands that knew how best to wield it – her hands, a warrior's hands, last of many generations of warriors – and they had broken the blade and blunted the edges. And then they had sent it out again, the poor blunt broken thing, and hoped that it would work as well as it had done before. Stark knew differently. She had seen the response of *seaQuest*'s commander to that one torpedo: try to run away. If that was the best that UEO could do, they'd be better advised to pull some Nor-Pac pigboat captain out of retirement and drop him into the Bridge Chair. At least he might not turn tail after the first exchange of fire.

There was a knock on the frame of the open hatchway that opened into her cramped quarters, and Stark flicked the photograph into a drawer and out of sight. 'Come,' she said, and watched Maxwell step across the threshold. He moved like a man entering a lion's den. That was just as it should be. 'Anything yet?'

The sensor chief shook his head. 'Long range sonar still shows nothing. They're not coming after us.'

Stark uttered a derisive laugh. 'They will. That's their mission. Whether they have full propulsion, whether they have weapons or not – they've got to try to stop us in any way possible. That's the UEO mandate.'

She reached up to the bookshelves built into the head of her bunk, pulled out a thick volume, glanced casually at it and then tossed it onto the low table at Maxwell's side. Its impact was like a gunshot, and she saw him jump at the sound. Her lip curled scornfully. To think that this … this thing was the best of her present crew. She looked back at the photograph, at all the bright, hopeful, enthusiastic faces. Maxwell was there too. All of them were there. All of them …

'*I* could have commanded her as a peacekeeper. It should have been a Stark. *That* would've been my entrée into the history books. First commander of the UEO peacekeeper *seaQuest*. Instead I'm the first Stark to be relieved of command. The first Stark *disgraced* ...'

Her eyes went distant, dull and emotionless as any shark's. 'What I did that day – *tried* to do that day – at the Livingston Trench, wasn't just for me. It was for all of you – my *crew*. And they all bore witness against me. Their *Captain*. All except you, Mr Maxwell ...'

She had not expected a response to the compliment, because it had been nothing more than a statement of fact. For all his keeping faith, for all his being the best aboard the *Delta*, he had been nothing like the best aboard the *seaQuest*. But the worst honest man among traitors and mutineers has to be the best, otherwise the world stops making sense. There were occasions when Stark thought that her world, and her future in it, had stopped making sense a long time ago; and then there were times, like now, when all the sense came back.

When the *seaQuest* came back, and gave her a chance to recover her proper command – or take it away from anyone else forever.

'Captain,' said Maxwell, reluctant as always to break into her dreamy moments. She glanced at him, and gave him as much attention as he deserved. 'I don't mean to question you, but the crew's – They don't understand why we're provoking this fight.'

Stark raised her hand and he fell silent at once. She shook her head. 'This "crew", as you call them, were nothing more than a ragtag bunch of mercenaries with a broken-down ship and no one to run it before *I* came on board.'

He knew that; they all knew that. And they didn't like it. Marilyn Stark didn't care whether they liked it or not, so long as her orders were obeyed without question. And if they weren't ... Pollack had learned the answer to that, and in learning, had taught the others as well.

'I organized them, I gave them a sense of purpose, and now they want me to run? Well, I won't do it! Not as long as *seaQuest* is out there. You tell them we'll satisfy their petty greed and pirate all the colonies they want ... *after* we complete *my* mission. After whatever incompetent the UEO's brought on to command *my* ship either radios his surrender, or rides her down into the abyss ...'

NINE

Gedrick Power Station was still little more than a confusion of twisted piping and perforated containment chambers that would take heavy equipment a couple of months to clear, but the worst eco-threat was over. One by one, the swarm of TeamCraft and welder-crabs that had been fussing around the main derrick and its damaged vent pulled back towards the *seaQuest*. The uncontrolled billowing of waste gases had been reduced to no more than a thin, dirty plume in the water, and as the last TeamCraft was silhouetted by the actinic flare of its welding-torch, even that feather of poisonous filth dwindled to nothing. The TeamCraft crew laid another patch, just for luck; then disengaged and headed gratefully for home.

*

Commander Ford leaned over the communications console. Chief O'Neill was running another systems diagnostic check, the third so far, and he watched lights glow and screens flicker with the mild half-interest of a man with nothing better to do. The inactivity chafed at him, and it was made plain in the way he paced up and down the Bridge, peering at duty stations while managing to keep himself from actually interfering. The past few hours had dragged by for everyone aboard the *seaQuest*, all the more so because only Engineering had been able to get out and *do* something. Then O'Neill blinked at something he heard, muttered a request for verification into the live mike, smiled quickly and handed the headset up to him.

Looking dubious, Ford held it to his ear, listened for a few seconds; and then a slow grin began to spread over his face. He nodded as the message repeated, dropped the headset back into O'Neill's hands, and hurried across to where Captain Bridger was staring thoughtfully at a screenful of data.

'Sir,' he said, 'they've done it.' The grin was still there, and getting wider, as if he'd been able to play a part in the repair operation after all. And he had, in a manner of speaking anyway; if *seaQuest* hadn't been there, such a fast repair would not have been possible. '*We've* done it. The patching is complete.'

Bridger had looked up as the Exec approached, and now was gazing thoughtfully at him as he made the brief report. Ford had a sudden creepy sensation of *déjà vu*, because Captain Stark had used to go off into those same fits of silence, staring straight through you as if you weren't there. Or were there, and weren't important. That had been worse.

His words seemed to go right past Bridger as though they hadn't registered, and there was no change in his expression. Certainly it didn't show any of the satisfaction that the Exec was feeling. He had hoped for some sort of response, but this ... this was disturbing. The Captain was probably still brooding over the renegade *Delta*, and about not being able to do anything about it. He could understand that.

Then Bridger cleared his data screen and stood up. 'Very good,' he said. 'Meanwhile, be so kind as to call Doctor Westphalen and Lieutenant Hitchcock to the wardroom: and let's go down there ourselves. I think,' he said in a low, confidential voice, 'I've found it.'

'The virus?'

'Better than that. Our saboteur.'

*

Nathan sat at the table, his hands folded, and looked at the other three. He had been wary, because the information in front of him could have been a double bluff, intended to lead anyone who went looking for information down half-a-dozen wrong deductive turns. Ford was a member of the original crew, one who could have been set up – or who could as easily have set *himself* up, the injured innocent, the man in the wrong place at the wrong time – who had been in the right place all along. Bridger shook his head, trying to shake that sort of tangled thinking back to where it belonged, in the garbage-heap of discarded ideas at the back of his mind. It was like espionage: once you started distrusting everybody, it was almost impossible to stop.

He dragged himself back to reality with an effort and studied the screen, trying to get beyond the pixels of the display, trying to get inside the mind of the calm, closed face that stared back at him, knowing where all that crooked thinking had originated.

'I went back through all the system service logs from a year ago,' he said. 'Nothing unusual. So I checked the daily inspection sheets and personnel manifest for that same period. The *seaQuest* was in dock at the time, with a minimal crew.'

'So?' Ford said.

'So the manifest shows one senior officer on board during that entire period.' He touched a control on the table in front of him. On the briefing screen at the end of the room, a picture of a woman came up. A woman in the uniform and rank-tabs of a captain. The Navy's ID mugshot didn't do justice to Marilyn Stark's coldly attractive features; but it had managed to catch something that Ford had probably become all too familiar with during his first tour of duty on the *seaQuest*. There was a shuttered, icy control in that face, a locking-in of more pressure than a human being should be expected to bear. Many captains became increasingly reserved as they moved up through the ranks, and as their security clearances forced them to become ever more reticent about what they knew. That was what had prompted Nathan Bridger to propose what had become the Old Man program. Officers with that much power, with that much knowledge shut inside their heads and no way to release it, could become ... strange. The face on the screen had that look.

'Stark,' Ford said under his breath. Not quietly enough.

'You served under her, didn't you?' said Nathan. He knew well enough, but it was always best to have confirmation in matters like this.

Ford nodded. 'I ... I was her Ex-O at Livingston Trench.' He watched at the picture on the screen, then looked down at his own hands resting on the desk, raising them a little to study his fingers, watching for any trace of tremor. There was none. 'She was relieved of command. No demotion ... All the same, Nor-Pac Command recommended psychiatric evaluation. But she refused. And then, one day, she was just gone. Disappeared ...' He shrugged, and shook his head. 'You would have to know her, sir ... know about her *family*, to understand. She – she's good.'

Bridger caught a strange tinge of sadness in the gesture, and felt himself liking Ford even more. Definitely a good officer, if he could sympathize with someone like that. Because even though she would reject it and resent the offer, Marilyn Stark deserved sympathy. 'I do know her,' he said. 'And how good she is. She should be. I taught her.'

Westphalen stared at him. 'You?'

'She was a cadet of mine at the Academy. I was her sponsor when she applied for her officer's bars.' *Is that what hurts inside you, Captain Nathan Bridger? Knowing that if you had made your doubts known, if you had withheld that sponsorship, then ...*

'... Her first command was a surface ship serving in the North Atlantic. There was a skirmish, and she fired first.' It was a habit with the Stark family. 'Two deaths resulted.' He breathed in, breathed out, looked at Ford, at all of them, but didn't really see any faces except for the ones that weren't there. 'One of them was my son ...'

'And now she's after *you*?' asked Hitchcock dubiously. Nathan came back with a little shudder that he turned into a shake of the head.

'No. I'm accidental. She's after the *seaQuest*.'

'Sir,' said Ford, 'I can't believe she'd deliberately destroy her own ship.'

'That's exactly why she wants to destroy it. If she can't have it, nobody can. And besides – if there's no *seaQuest*, her renegades and the others like them will own the sea.' He grinned at them, a hard, tough expression that went better with his uniform than he probably knew himself. 'What she didn't count on was a ...' The grin broadened as he glanced at Hitchcock. 'A "tourist" on board. One whose knowledge predates hers.' He tapped the desk-top, drawing little arcs and circles with the tip of one finger. 'I've been thinking that maybe we're going at this wrong. That maybe instead of attacking the virus we should –' the finger made a quick, curving sweep, '– go around it.'

'It might work,' muttered Hitchcock. Her eyes were unfocussed, and Nathan guessed she was studying schematics on a screen inside her own head, considering options. 'You probably wouldn't have full propulsion and weapons, but ...'

'Anything's better than what we've got.' There was one other person on board that Stark wouldn't have anticipated when she laid her little traps. The Wolenczak boy. He might be a self-centered little creep sometimes, but so far as computers were concerned ... 'Coordinate things with Lucas.'

'Yes, sir.' Hitchcock whisked out, looking happier about things than she had done for a long time. Doctor Westphalen looked anything but.

'*Weapons*,' she snapped. 'That's what all this is really about, isn't it?'

Nathan Bridger allowed himself a single grunt of impatience at the bloody-minded attitude which by now should have been set aside. There was a time and a place for everything – but not this, not here, and not now. 'No,

Doctor,' he said. 'It's about saving lives. Now let's get to work ...!'

*

Bridger stepped quietly out into the passageway that ran down from the docking bay. He felt weary; no, he felt *exhausted*, as though talking about his son, and thus supposedly unburdening himself of some of the weight of grief, had taken far more effort than saying nothing. But still: it had been said, and the three to whom he had spoken would perhaps have a better understanding now of why he had no desire ever again to sit in the captain's chair — at least, for any longer than it took to get them out of this present mess. Enough understanding at least to stop hounding, to just let matters rest.

Rest ... The thought was an appealing one. And not just to Bridger. During the short briefing, if that was what it had really been, the repair teams had all come back to *seaQuest* and he met them now, trailing along the passageway by ones and twos, dirty, bedraggled and dog-tired. So tired that they didn't even have the satisfaction of a good job well done. That would come later, after a few hours' sleep, a wash, a bite to eat; all the things they needed to make them feel human again, rather than small, insignificant parts of the machinery they had been fighting for so long. But there was one thing that he found encouraging.

Like the pair who had struggled out of their flooded TeamCraft, the repair crews had been a mixture of science and military personnel. There had been no time, and fortunately no real inclination, to separate them out. They were separating now, just a bit; the beige suits and the black suits were tending to drift apart, re-joining their own people. But not all of them. A couple of the military crewmen were talking to a trio of scientists, and neither side seemed in too much of a hurry to break off the conversation. Shared tension, shared risk; all of a sudden there was common ground where none had been before. And shared scruffiness. Nathan was too polite to point out that both groups were equally grimy, equally sweaty, and except for the color of their jumpsuits and the length of their hair, they weren't easy to tell apart. In all sorts of ways, it was a start.

He headed for the Bridge first. He and Ford spent some time there, with other crew members who would need to be involved, hanging over Hitchcock's station and examining the systems schematics in question. Hitchcock, of course, knew where all the changes and additions were, but the rest of the ship she knew mostly from schematic: whereas Nathan knew it from the guts up, having seen the guts put in. *And this is where she went wrong*, Nathan thought, pointing out the best 'weak spots' to his eager pupils. *Stark thinks that the people here will be trying to fix the problem in the software ... not the hardware ... and even if they tried some drastic rerouting with the hardware, they wouldn't know it well enough to do it* fast. *But there's someone on board who does know it that well. Bad luck for Stark –*

'There,' Nathan said, 'and there, and there and there. Take those off the computer entirely, run 'em off whatever you like, laptops, scientific calculators, I don't care – then *those* conduits to *those*, don't go near the mains whatever you do or the computer'll sense the change and reroute them into the main network, and everything'll all get screwed up again. Just run the cables down the damn passageways, we're not trying for the school neatness award here –'

Under the officers' directions, teams began to fan out through *seaQuest* and do things to her systems wiring that would have given most of her design team hives. The erstwhile chief of the design team was here, though, and had decided that hives were much preferable to being dead. In three or four corridors, one after another, combined science and Navy teams were going out to engage in constructive sabotage. The Navy crew would lead the way down, studying a printout, hunting a specific panel: they would find it, and another of the military crew would pull a panel tool and pop the fascia off. Then the science crew would lean in and start to work, unfastening the fastened and mating connections that had never been intended to be mated, pulling out the visceral-looking cabling, the fat ribbed sheaths of fibre optic and wire, dissecting them apart like mad mechanical surgeons, then splicing them to thick jury-rigged cable-bundles that went snaking down the corridors like so much errant gut –

Elsewhere the surgery was even more drastic. The galley, snugged right against the side of the inner hull, was one spot briefly disrupted by the teams; cans and bottles back in the cool store were swept off their shelves, and one of the military crew leaned over the shelving and went at the supporting bulkhead with a small power saw. The knitted cyclic-polymer surface gave like skin, splitting under the saw to let the insulating 'bray' oil inside ooze out like blood. Once the incision was finished, and cloths had been put down to catch the leakage, science crew members reached in and started pulling out more of the visceral-looking conduits and tubing: they tumbled out shining onto the cover-sheets, and the resections and splicing began again, while the galley staff looked on in annoyance and went about restacking their cans elsewhere ...

There was nothing more Nathan could do to help accomplish what they had to. However, there had been something niggling at his mind for an hour or two now: he went to see what could be done about *that*.

*

'I was going to come see you,' Lucas said, barely looking up from his keyboard as Nathan came in. 'We've got a problem. The sabotage isn't fully integrated.'

'Come again?'

'There's not enough code in the main system to make it work,' Lucas said, with exaggerated patience. 'The routines being guarded by the "watchdogs" are only partial. There has to be a kernel hidden somewhere else – a "core routine" with the basic instructions that set the whole thing in motion – because I haven't found anything like that in the main system, and it has to be *somewhere*.'

' "Kernel"? Are we talking about nuts now?' Bridger muttered.

'Listen,' Lucas said, 'use your brains. Stark's not really a programmer –'

'What *you* would call a programmer,' Nathan said.

Lucas smiled slightly and kept tapping at his keyboard. 'Except for down and dirty practical stuff. She's a tech, a competent tech, at best. And she's not an engineer. She doesn't know this ship well enough to wind a routine of nested viruses into the existing code without leaving tracks like a four-by-four in the snow. And think about it – even if she did, somebody woulda caught her at it. It'd take too much time. There were enough people aboard *seaQuest* to have noticed what she was up to.'

'So?' Nathan said.

'So she would have done her work privately, on media that she could conceal, and that wouldn't have left any trace of her work in the main computers ... the diagnostics would have picked it up if she'd worked there. She would have recorded her code in some self-perpetuating form, and then put it aside somewhere, where it could feed into the main systems and keep reminding them how they were supposed to be subverted –'

'So that even if we found the "subversive" code,' Nathan said, 'it would still be lying doggo somewhere in the systems, in hardware. And a while later, her installation would restore it – and we would be as badly off as before. The same crap would start all over again.'

Lucas bestowed on Nathan the warm smile reserved for backward students who are finally catching on. Nathan withheld, for the moment, his reaction to it. 'Right,' Lucas said. 'So somewhere in the ship she left a media reader hooked into the computer network. It would mimic the "tell-me-three-times" backups that some computers use, and it'd feed its burnt-in instructions into the computer net once every, oh, twelve hours – maybe even twenty-four hours if she was concerned about it being noticed, or felt sure no one would look.'

'That sounds about right, I think,' Nathan said.

'Okay. So all *you* have to do is answer the question: where would she hide something like that?'

'Where no one would look –' Nathan bit his lip. 'Unless

she was a fan of the Purloined Letter school of hiding things. In plain sight —'

He thought about that for a moment. It would suit one aspect of Stark's personality as he remembered it, the delight in pulling one over, obviously, insultingly, on those not smart enough to keep up with her. But that kind of trick she reserved for those whom she considered might possibly be her peers. She would not think that way about the present crew of *seaQuest*. She would consider them peons, and not waste more time than was necessary on fooling them.

'Non-maintenance areas,' Bridger said. 'Or minimal-maintenance ones. I think I have a few ideas where to start.'

'It'll be small, and something that won't make much of a power signature,' Lucas said. 'She wouldn't be dumb enough to give herself away by producing waveform where there shouldn't be any.'

'Right,' Nathan said, and looked over Lucas's shoulder at the screen, still showing page after page of indecipherable code, tangles of mathematical symbols, barbed-wire nests of parentheses. 'How're you doing?'

'Got my first couple of bypasses,' Lucas said. He was visibly breaking into a sweat as he studied the screen. 'They won't be any good until they're all done, though: they run in parallel and reinforce each other. And if you don't find her little dog-in-the-manger, they won't be any good anyway. I wouldn't put it past her to have told her routine to refresh the system more frequently after our trouble started.'

Nathan nodded.

'I found something in my quarters —' he said.

Lucas's face sealed over. 'Later,' he said. 'I mean, I wouldn't mind a chat, but if some cranky chick's programming kills me, I am going to be *very* annoyed –'

He has a point there, Nathan thought, and went away.

TEN

Minutes later Bridger was scrambling down a vertical companionway, whistling – not so much from good cheer, as to defuse his own nervousness. Down here, though, it could well have been mistaken for whistling in the dark to keep the boogeyman away. Looking around him in an attempt to get his bearings, he doubted that any self-respecting boogeyman would have come anywhere near the place. *seaQuest* might have been the pride of the fleet, the right of the line and all the rest of that junk, but she was a seagoing vessel and like all other seagoing vessels, she had a bilge. Officially this was the submarine's keel deck, but he knew a bilge when he saw it. And smelt it.

The place had started out as a standard passageway like those farther up towards civilization, but after that it had been heavily redecorated by someone with a taste for pipes and conduits, recessed panels and openwork deck grids. *Post-industrial chic*, thought Bridger, rubbing his hands together and wondering if they would ever be completely free of grease again. What hadn't struck him previously – but did now – was how *long* this passageway seemed: under the present circumstances, it seemed that if he looked down it long enough, he would perceive the curvature of the earth. *And I have to search this for something little?*

I think I need a smaller boat ...

He sighed and strode off along the passageway, being cautious about how he moved across the metal deck. With all the oily slime and time-expired grease that had accumulated down here since *seaQuest*'s launch, it would be all too easy to find that his feet were going one way and his head the other – and none of those pipes were likely to be kind to an unprotected human skull.

He walked a while – and then he saw it. Not quite where his memory had claimed he left it, but close enough. The panel was marked COMMUNICATIONS, but the clarity of that label had been somewhat degraded by several layers of the grime that had worked past and over it on the way to the bilge. *The obvious place,* he thought. *More to the point ... the insulting place. Even if I'm wrong, best to get it out of the way first.*

Bridger stood on tip-toe in an attempt to reach the panel, and felt the first warning slither from under the sole of one shoe. He came warily back down to an even keel again, breathing hard and holding tightly to a shoulder-high pipe just in case he really did slip. Then he looked at the pipe and gazed thoughtfully at the others running by at ankle-height, knee-height – in fact, at all the heights that might come in useful for a man reaching higher up a bulkhead than he was able. They had another advantage: some of them had been hot, or ran hot intermittently, and what was a lethally-slippery film of oil on the deck had baked into a hard crust that looked like a cross between crude plastic and failed taffy. There was little else to recommend it, but – he checked carefully before trusting his full weight to the boost upwards – it wasn't slippery.

Of course, when Nathan got level with the panel, he found that it had rusted shut. *All this oil about the place, and it rusts. That's just great.* It took three solid punches with the heel of his hand to pop the latch, but to his relief the actual lid swung open with no further need for persuasion. Inside was so much of the usual circuitry and braids of colorcoded spaghetti that he began to doubt whether he had even opened the right box. *Take the money next time,* thought Nathan drily, then remembered the flashlight in his pocket. Never go anywhere without a penlight, a knife and a box of matches. Well, he had the light at any rate. If its batteries weren't dead ...

They weren't. The little penlight wasn't about to dazzle anyone with its brilliance, a bit like some people he could name, but it was bright enough for his purposes. One of which was holding it in his mouth. The aluminum barrel clanked unpleasantly against his teeth, with a metallic flavor and a sourly acid backtaste that suggested the batteries might not be dead, but they were certainly leaking. Given that the alternative was to have only one hand free instead of two, and that while balanced on a rickety conduit three feet above a metal deck, Bridger went with having a nasty taste in his mouth.

Rummaging among the wires took only a few seconds; it was only too easy to rummage that little bit too hard and get a shock or disconnect something vital, but Nathan Bridger – *the* Nathan Bridger – was as much at ease poking around in the electrical entrails of his own ship as young Lucas seemed to be picking the brains of its computers. And then he saw it. The little metal container was buried well back, small and demure and plain-looking … and it was nothing that belonged here among the organic-looking conduits and cables. He reached in, and finding that it was … just, just … within reach without needing to be pulled off its mounting, Bridger popped the container's cover and gazed in satisfaction at the wires and circuits packed inside. His attention was particularly drawn to the little block of solid-state equipment: a RAM solid, low-power, not active at the moment.

He extended one index finger, pushed it into the container, made a beckoning hook – and jerked the finger out. Several wires obediently followed, and after that came a small whining noise like that of a frustrated insect. So far so good. Straightening the finger again, he poked it at the only button visible on the casing. Out of a thin slit at the back of the casing popped a disc of shiny silver refracting plastic, thin as a sheet of paper, no bigger than an egg yolk. He just caught it by the edges as it came out, and slipped it into his breast pocket: possibly it was something Lucas could use. There were no other slots, no other discs that he could see.

It was pleasant, though, to have these few seconds alone down in the bowels of the ship, hearing nothing but the rumble of the propulsion systems and the powerplant, the ship's heartbeat; a moment of peace, no voices, no crisis, no trouble. Heaven only knew what was going on up on the Bridge, but it wasn't his problem, not right this minute.

Nathan breathed out softly. It was really a pain in the ass – having all the subtleties of the ship he had designed, all the systems he had intended to make life easier, effortless, for a crew, now making them more difficult – turning out, in fact, to be an Achilles heel. *Something for the drawing board next time*, he thought, while in the back of his brain, something screamed, *What 'next time'??!* Nathan ignored it. *A non-subversible backup for the submersible. Systems that can't be suborned because they're too* simple *to suborn –*

Next time? he thought. *Am I nuts? What 'next time'?*

No time for that now, though. Cautiously he went back the way he had come, concentrating on not slipping in the oil. Up above him, matters would be coming to a head. He would be needed.

His mind went back to the sun on the blue water, and the place where no one had particularly needed him except Darwin –

– and to his shock, he found himself enjoying this even more.

Frowning, Nathan scrambled back up to deck level.

*

On the Bridge, Bridger stood at the Navigation table, going over projected maps of the region with Ford, when O'Neill called over from his station, 'Captain, I've got her!'

'The *Delta*?' Bridger said, as they headed over to him.

'Yes, sir.' O'Neill said, working over the console. 'I'm picking up a low-band signal. A deep ocean housing facility. The renegade sub is there, attacking. The colonists are trying to fight it off with some of their minisubs ...' He paused for a second, listening, while Nathan and Ford looked at each other. Then O'Neill looked up, concerned, and said, 'It doesn't sound like it's working ...'

Nathan's mouth compressed. *Not again. Not now. Just a little while more is all we need –*

– and overhead, the lights flickered, dipped down to

almost nothing – then, for the first time in hours, came up to full again. There was a sort of restrained cheer from the Bridge crew, and Ford looked at Nathan with great approval.

'Good boy,' Nathan said, thinking of the hands flashing over a keyboard elsewhere on the ship. To Hitchcock, now working over her station at double speed to take inventory, he said, 'What sort of propulsion do we have?'

'One quarter normal,' she said, sounding triumphant. 'But still no weapons or defenses ...'

Wonderful, Nathan thought. 'Well, Mr Ford. Suggestions?'

Ford didn't respond right away. Finally he looked up and said softly, 'I don't believe this one's in the manual either ...'

Oh joy, Nathan thought, and knew what Ford was thinking: *time for you to take command* ... He opened his mouth to put the idea back where it belonged. Then he stopped – for a glance around the Bridge told him that every eye was on him, waiting to see what he would say – and in all those eyes was a very obvious hope. The expressions were all those of people waiting for *his* orders ... and all he had to do was say the word.

Nathan tried hard to think of some excuse *not* to take command ... and could not. *Horrible,* he thought. *But there are too many lives riding on this now. Ford is right, dammit.*

I hate *this!*

Nathan sighed ... then said to Ford, 'Feed coordinates to Navigation and plot a course, Mr Ford ...'

Ford's smile was tight and glad. '*Yes sir* ...' he said, and turned back to the Navigations table to bring up the fastest of the courses they had been examining. Nathan turned to watch the front screens, and felt that weight descending on him, the weight he had not wanted to feel. He stood straight against it and kept his face quiet: his reactions to this situation were now his own business, not the crew's — he now had their morale and reactions to think about as well as his own.

From outside, the WSKRs relayed to the screens their multiple views of *seaQuest*: now coming to life, lights coming on sparkling along her hull, and slowly, heeling a bit over to starboard and easing forward, away from Gedrick and out into the dark waters in the shadow of the Long Chain Mountains. She leaned upward and southward, heading for one of the gaps in the Long Chain, for the deep research facility that had called for help.

Bridger watched her move out, graceful even on such low power, and hoped that they would have time to finish the work they had to before they caught up with the attacker. Otherwise ...

And there was no otherwise.

ELEVEN

Even a quarter of *seaQuest*'s normal available thrust was no crawl. She swept along through the waters on the far side of the Long Chain, making depth and building her momentum. Ahead of her, Loner surveyed the path, matching found terrain to mapped terrain, relaying what it saw and storing new data for current scan and later improvements of the maps of this area. Behind it, Mother came along, checking Loner's data and compiling it with side-looking sonar, while running *en-passant* checks on the mineral content of the bottom terrain. In the rear, Junior hurried to keep up, acting as eyes-behind and monitoring the water above them for signs of any other craft in the area – not just the *Delta*: it could be inconvenient for deep-draft ships if a submarine battle broke out directly underneath them.

Inside *seaQuest* herself, the desperate business of hardware rerouting of circuitry and systems was still going on at best possible speed. Half the ship looked like a careless gastroenterologist had been conducting surgery on the run: the thick gut-looking conduits now lay down both longitudinal corridors, and reached up in ugly and hap-hazard-looking fashion to wall panels, up into ceiling vents, down into hatches on the floors beside the cetacean tubes. It was a mess – but increasingly, it was becoming a working mess.

Or so Nathan desperately hoped. He stood in the middle of the Bridge, watching the science and military crew work feverishly to make the last systems connections to the Bridge consoles. Fat conduits were running all over the place, so that you could trip and break your neck if you weren't careful, and all the watertight doors had had to be overridden: one more thing to think about, for if the fighting suddenly got bad and the ship took hits enough to start letting water again, the only way to seal her up would be by literally cutting off their newly-resumed control of ship's systems. Nathan tried not to worry about this prospect more than he had to ... though the problem ticked along in the back of his head, insisting that it could yet need a solution: right now, having to seal up compartments would amount to suicide.

Now Nathan leaned over O'Neill's comms console, watching him monitor the messaging that was coming in from the housing facility. They were 'hopscotching' their available transmitters, using several of them in series and switching hurriedly from one to another, probably to keep the *Delta* from guessing which one was being used, and taking that one out. It was a wise move, for if the rogue sub wanted to shut down the facility's comms entirely, it would have to target *everything* that looked as if it might be a transmitter, and that would take plenty of time, and use up crucial weaponry. *Smart people*, Nathan thought. *Hang on, just hang on a little while longer: we're coming –*

O'Neill was following the housing facility's transmission from frequency to frequency, frowning at the difficulty of the chase, but at the same time, enjoying the challenge of it. 'They're using everything from Q-band to low-band to null-prop to orange juice cans and string,' he said, sending his board into another run of scan mode to pick up the facility's latest shift of frequency. 'God knows what the attacking sub must think – possibly even that their comms are iffy, and that the colony's messages might not be getting through.' He grinned a little. 'Good for us if they think so.'

'They'll be furious if they think that,' Bridger said. 'I'm betting that the rogue desperately *wants* those messages to get through. Otherwise we won't come ... and then where are they? All dressed up and no one to party with ...'

O'Neill smiled grimly. 'Well, if they get careless and don't watch their butts while they're hammering that place –'

Bridger shook his head, finding the possibility minimal. 'I don't think we can count on that,' he said softly. 'I wish to God we could, but what that ship's commander wants more than anything else is the sight of us –'

O'Neill stopped, then, and listened intently. 'More of the colonists' mini-subs are amassing now, sir. Trying to block the –' Then he caught himself. '*Delta-IV has fired!*'

'Two torpedoes away,' Ortiz said, and paused. '– Impact. Two direct strikes!'

'Upping the ante,' Nathan muttered. He had been afraid this would happen: yet another massacre of the innocents. Ford hurried over to him; Nathan turned. 'Talk to me, Mr Ford.'

Ford did not look like a man bearing good news. 'We've

recovered minimal weapons control,' he said. 'Tube number one only. With *manual* firing capability only.'

Not great, but sure as hell better than nothing, Nathan thought. *A helluva lot better than what we had a couple of hours ago ...* 'What about the targeting?' he said.

'Targeting systems are still down,' said Ford.

Bridger frowned hard. 'So,' he said, 'we may be able to fire *one* torpedo *manually* – but we have no means of telling it where to go ...'

Ford nodded, looking unhappier yet.

Nathan stood there and considered, turned to pace ... and found himself looking at the Bridge tank, Darwin's 'station'. Darwin was hanging there, idle but interested, watching him, waiting. *I am going to get* you *out of this, if no one else,* Nathan thought, and turned away. *None of this is* your *fault.*

He tried to concentrate. *Think laterally, Danielson always said. Because thinking linearly is what your opponent expects: nine times out of ten, it's the best* he *can do ... and he won't suspect you of something he can barely conceive of himself ...*

Nathan found himself being dreadfully thankful that Marilyn Stark had never had much time for the Old Man. It was one of the things about her that had caused comment among the cadets of her year, who by and large practically worshipped Danielson. Stark, Nathan had heard, had found him 'inefficient' – too warm, that was taken to mean: for Stark herself had usually been referred to by the other cadets as 'the Snow Queen'. At the time, Nathan had thought it was just envy for her admittedly brilliant scholastic and military performance. Now, though, he knew otherwise. A cold mind, that one, very fixed, very disciplined and focussed: but that very focus could turn out to be Stark's weak spot, and exploitable. A collimated laser beam is unquestionably brighter than an uncollimated spot – but a spotlight shows you what's going on around the perimeter of a point, as well as at the point itself. Stark's very fixedness could well blind her, narrowing her preparations and confining them to options that her prejudiced world view would make her consider likely or possible. The unlikely or seemingly impossible would be ignored ...

Our only advantage, Nathan thought: *that I know she's there, but she doesn't know I'm here. God, I hope it's enough ...*

Which still left Nathan with his biggest problem: targeting. *How do you hit your target when you've got no way to tell the torpedo where to go to?* ... The nasty truth of it was that Stark had hardly needed to bother with the damage to the computer control of *seaQuest*'s propulsion systems: removing targeting ability left her helpless to do anything but ram. For a brief second Nathan considered that. Even out the odds, ram the *Delta*'s sail and take out the command center beneath it: would the damage *seaQuest* would incur be a fair enough trade? How many of the crew would die? How many of their passengers? ...

You're crazy even to think she would ever let you get that close to her boat, he thought. *And anyway, it's too linear a response ... she'll be expecting you to consider it. No, try something else ...*

Nathan paced away from the Command chair again, staring at the floor. *If only there were a way to circumvent the computer's own targeting routines – but there's not: the virus is planted more securely in and around those routines than anywhere else, or so Lucas said. Stark took the route of least effort with that – and the most elegant route: even if we did recover a torpedo or two, she knows they'll be useless.* Nathan laughed soundlessly, a bitter under-his-breath 'hah', as he came back to the Command chair again, turned his back on it, stared at the back of the Bridge. *She's succeeding even as we think we're beating her – making us waste our time on repairs that won't really help. Damn her!* He walked toward the back of the Bridge, past Ford, who was looking at him with concern again. *Pity we can't just program a torpedo to hit anything that looks like a* Delta. He laughed again, this time at the way his desperation was beginning to manifest as lunacy. *Why stop there? Pity we can't just paint a big target on the* Delta, *and the words 'Open Here', and tell the torpedo, 'Sic 'em' –*

He stood there, unfocussed, then looked at the tank at the back of the Bridge, and at Darwin again … and the idea formed. On the instant, Nathan hated himself for having it: but it would work, and there was nothing else to do. At least, nothing that he could conceive and execute in time.

Bridger turned quickly back to Ford. 'Do our present torpedoes have manual tracking options?'

'Sir?' Ford said, surprised.

'I mean, can we program them to lock on a designated frequency?'

'If we need to,' Ford said, still looking bemused, 'certainly. Radio transmissions, or …' Then he followed Bridger's glance to look over at Darwin, in the tank … and slowly Ford's eyes lit with the idea.

'We can "tag" her –!' he said.

'Keep me in the loop,' Nathan said. 'This shouldn't take too long.'

He left the Bridge, and Darwin went after him.

*

169

It was some minutes before he got to the sea deck, and when he did, he found Westphalen there before him. Inside his head, Nathan said several very bad words: this was not an interview he particularly wanted to have anyone else witness. But he would feel as guilty about throwing Westphalen out of it, as he felt about the interview itself ...

Darwin's head was up out of the pool on the sea deck, and looked over toward the doorway.

'Hello!' he said.

'He told me he was waiting for you.' Westphalen said, looking at Nathan, and at what he carried, with quiet concern.

Bridger stood there in the doorway, full of feelings so mixed that he was nearly paralyzed. He hadn't said a word, had barely come in: but here was Darwin, cheerful and ready, as if he had been expecting him. *And he might have been*, Nathan thought guiltily. *I haven't been paying much attention to the access tubes on the Bridge, or the tank there – it's still so hard to believe they're there at all – that whole aspect of the design was one I never thought they would really take seriously. All the same – how long has he been watching me, wondering what's going on?*

And has he been wondering? He has access to ship's communications through the translator, Lucas tells me. If he's wanted to, he'll have been listening to everything that's been going on. Though how much he understands of it, I can't be sure ...

The rebreather harness he was holding was heavy: Nathan had to pass it to the other hand. Darwin's glance followed it with interest, then went back to Nathan's face. *How much does he understand of my expression-changes, I wonder? Does he even know they mean anything? ... Oh, I hate this whole thing, I hate it –*

'Island,' Darwin said, 'play!'

'Yes,' Nathan said. 'I want to play too – but this isn't going to be like the other games we had ... though boy, do I wish it were. Darwin, I need your help.'

'Help?' Darwin said immediately. 'Darwin help.' That cheerful tone of voice again, absolutely ready for anything. *If he were human, he'd be a Boy Scout ...*

Nathan shook his head. 'You might want to hear what it is first ...' *Mostly because it could kill you – !*

Darwin put his head up on the edge of the coping, looking up and a little sideways at Nathan. 'Trust – Bridger,' the dolphin said.

Nathan was rocked to his core. The easy trust made him feel more guilty than ever, and he wondered how much detail Lucas's vocabulary program had given the dolphin on the concept. 'That's my problem,' Bridger said unhappily. 'I almost wish you didn't.' *But the lives of all the people on this ship are on the line. Both the crew, who know the risks – and the civilians, who never asked for them, who're trusting us to save their lives. And his life, too. There's no way out of this. Whatever needs doing, has to be done – even the possible sacrifice of an innocent, for the other innocents –* Nathan did his best to swallow the lump in his throat. '– And I'll hold Bill Noyce personally responsible if *anything* happens to you,' he said.

Darwin looked at him, saying nothing. It could be that he had no idea what Nathan's turmoil meant.

Then again, perhaps he *did* know – and, by keeping quiet, might be trying to leave Nathan his dignity. Who knew what passed for dignity among dolphins, or restraint?

But there was no time to deal with it now. Nathan knelt down on the coping, putting the rebreather harness down beside him. Off to the side, quietly, Westphalen said, 'We're at six hundred feet. It's at the limits of a dolphin's tolerance. The pressure alone —'

'He's done well over five hundred feet on the island,' Nathan said. 'No permanent aftereffects: he knows how to move to minimize the way the pressure works on his body.'

'Dive *deep*,' Darwin said. And was that pride in the synthesized voice? ... 'Hunt.'

'It's taking chances with his life,' Westphalen said.

The inward pain hit Nathan again. *Do you think I don't know that?* he wanted to shout, but instead he put the pain and the response forcefully aside, looking at Westphalen as challengingly as he could. 'Do you have another idea?'

She stood there looking at him, then shook her head, helpless. 'I wish I had ...'

Nathan looked from the rebreather to Darwin, and back again. 'Do you know what's out there, Darwin?' he said.

'Submarine,' Darwin said promptly. 'Ship that swims. Ship that *kills*.'

Now how much of this *is from Lucas's 'vocabulary' work?* Nathan wondered. 'Submarine,' he said, 'that's right.'

'Metal shark,' Darwin said, and for a moment the wicked teeth showed, and that eternal smile went very feral. 'Hunt.'

Nathan had to look across at Westphalen at that. She looked faintly shocked. They both knew how dolphins hated sharks and would hunt them down and kill them by ramming them with their beaks until they died of internal injuries.

'*Joke*,' Darwin said clearly, and laughed delphine laughter at them.

'He's learned metaphor,' Westphalen said, shocked. 'And humor!'

'Believe me, humor he had already,' Nathan said, grinning briefly. 'Shark imitations were part of his stock-in-trade. He'd sneak up behind you underwater and poke you in the back, then hang there laughing and grinning 'gotcha'. But as for the rest of it, I'm going to have a few words with that boy. Never mind. – Hunt, yeah, Darwin, that's the idea.'

'Deep,' Darwin said. 'Need air –' The tone was still completely cheerful and trusting: but he was looking at Nathan with an expression that suggested he wasn't sure how Nathan was going to help him on *this* one.

Nathan picked up the rebreather harness and beckoned the dolphin over. Calmly Darwin swam up to him, and rolled over in the water so that Nathan could start buckling the harness on.

It took a couple of minutes to get the rebreather onto Darwin – even when willing, a dolphin half out of water is a considerable bulk to wrestle into a harness of *any* shape. And the correct positioning of this one, especially the small gas exchange dome over the blowhole, the equivalent of a mouthpiece on a human's rebreather, was crucial: there must be absolutely no chance of letting it be knocked askew by movement or impact. Once the harness was cinched on snugly and the fastenings tightened, Nathan tried a few different ways to pull the rebreather out of kilter: the harness resisted, and the skin-latex seal around the blowhole stayed tight.

Darwin endured all this with an interested manner, eyeing Nathan as he finished up. 'This harness will let you breathe without having to surface,' Nathan said, as the dolphin slipped back down into the water, shook himself all over, like a man adjusting a jacket he'd just put on, and then put his head up again. 'It should feel no different from the sensor harness you wore back on the island.'

Darwin looked at Nathan as if he thought he had taken leave of his senses. 'Darwin *need* air,' he said, and this time the concern was audible. 'Too deep to go up fast –'

Nathan shook his head. 'You won't need to go up fast. You won't need to go up at *all*, with this.'

Darwin kept looking at him doubtfully. 'Joke?' he said. 'Not at all,' Nathan said. 'Go ahead – give it a try!'

Thoughtfully, Darwin ducked his head a little under the surface: Nathan, standing up to watch, saw the blowhole move, saw the dome over it cloud up with condensation as Darwin blew on purpose, and blew again, harder. It stayed in place. Then the dolphin submerged and swam a lap or so, carefully keeping a few feet under. Nathan watched him anxiously.

About thirty seconds later, Darwin came back up, and Nathan saw on him one of the expressions he knew dolphins *did* have: the jaw dropped open in surprise. '*Darwin breathe!*' the dolphin said delightedly.

Nathan had to smile despite himself, but the urge for amusement didn't last long. He hunkered down slowly by the edge of the pool once more and pulled the little device on its nylon strap out of his pocket, where it had been weighing like lead, both in his pants and on his conscience.

'All right,' he said to Darwin, 'you know what to do. When I open the tube, you go out and tag the marker. Remember? Like on the island.'

'Do,' Darwin said, and reached up eagerly out of the water for the strap.

Suddenly Westphalen was down beside them. 'Darwin,' she said softly, 'you don't *have* to do this if you don't want to.'

In other circumstances Nathan would have been annoyed with her: but now he had to agree that it was the right thing to say. Darwin looked at her very thoughtfully, slipped back down ... then upended and smacked the water with his tail, a gesture that Nathan recognized of old as one of absolute negation. 'No,' Darwin said. 'Hunt "shark". Do for Bridger.'

Nathan's insides clenched at the thought that anyone, anything, should do anything 'for *him*'. A long time, it had been, since any human being had said as much: a long lonely time now ...

The dolphin reached up again. Nathan turned the small targeting device over in his hands, uncapped the recessed switch, pressed the button there: the device began to cheep intermittently, and a small light on it began to blink. He capped it again, held it out. Darwin took the strap from him, biting down hard on it, and eyed Nathan sideways.

'Darwin swim like Bridger,' Darwin said merrily.

Nathan was bemused. 'Like me?' he said, and reached down to tap the rebreather, thinking the dolphin might be referring to Scuba or snorkeling gear.

Darwin's tail slapped the water. 'No suit,' he said, almost in Lucas's tone of voice, the clever explaining to the slow. 'Skin!'

And, laughing in dolphin, he dived, and was gone.

Bridger stood up next to Westphalen, smiling slightly. She stood too, looking rather confused. 'What was all that about?'

'Joke,' Nathan said, and headed out hurriedly, making for the Bridge.

TWELVE

On the Bridge, Ortiz looked up abruptly from his console as his WSKRs screens suddenly started to flicker with incoming fresh data. 'Approaching the flashpoint!' he said to Ford. 'Whiskers are picking up multiple small craft ... two thousand three hundred yards off our starboard bow!'

Bridger came in through the rear starboard door and his heart began to bang hard against his chest. The balloon was finally about to go up, and as usual, his insides were screaming, *We're not ready, we want a few minutes more to pull ourselves together* – 'Punch up the visual imaging on the forward screens,' Nathan said, making for the middle of the Bridge and doing his damndest to ignore his insides, for paying attention to them had never done him any good before ...

The screens came alive with the WSKR-imaged views of what most closely resembled an undersea prairie: though even this flatness was not unbroken – here and there across it stretched long, deep pressure trenches, doubtless the reason the housing facility was here in the first place – the mineral composition and fossil record of such places were of tremendous scientific and economic interest. The rolling foothills of the Long Chain Mountains were visible not too far away, and in the distance, visible to the WSKRs' systems if not to the naked eye, were the great mountains themselves, huge jagged peaks to make a mountaineer proud, some of them eighteen or maybe even nineteen thousand feet high: if they were much taller, they would have been islands. Down there in the prairie lay the housing facility, a smallish place by comparison to Gedrick, a cluster of bubbledomes and Quonset capsules linked by jury-rigged access tubes. Hovering around the perimeter of the place were about a dozen mini-subs of every imaginable kind of design – observation globes, little one-man, many-armed soil and rock sample retrievers, small crab-walking burrowers for digging up core samples: anything that could move around in the undersea environment and, however remotely, contribute to some kind of defence. Nathan's throat tightened at the sight of the fragile little craft, and at what faced them down: the *Delta*, floating there in silence, a great looming black bludgeon, silent, seemingly invulnerable, waiting ... waiting for *them*.

Nathan stood there looking at the thing with loathing. Once again the *Delta* had successfully called the shot, bringing them up from the depths to answer its threat to these innocents. *I've had about enough of this*, he thought. *Time to call some shots of my own.* 'Status, Mister Ford?'

'Weapons control reports tube one loaded, locked and standing by,' said Ford. 'Torpedo is fully charged.'

'Belay that,' said Nathan, shaking his head. 'Reduce the charge to twenty percent. I want to stop them, not destroy them.'

'Sir ... Aye-aye, sir.' Ford glanced at Phillips on the

weapons board. 'You heard the Captain. Twenty percent charge.' Though his tone of voice made it plain that he thought perhaps Nathan had returned to 'bee-bee-eyed' mode.

'Twenty percent aye,' said Phillips.

'That's all very well, sir,' Ford said quietly. 'But we don't have any of the automatics back on line down in the torpedo room, and a manual reload for any *second* shot will take between sixty and ninety seconds ...'

'So we get only one good shot,' Bridger said. 'Let's make it count.' Part of him was protesting, *It's not enough! We'll never make it work!* The rest of him was insisting, nearly as loudly, that it was still a lot more than they'd had earlier, he should count himself lucky and just get on with it –

'... But there's still no targeting,' Ford said.

Bridger sighed. 'One *bad* shot ...' he murmured. He was going to have to do it after all: what he had been praying he *wouldn't* have to. But there was no avoiding it now –

He swung around to the screens. The minisubs were moving again: *seaQuest*'s arrival had slowed them down, but only briefly. These were angry people, trying to defend what mattered to them – but *trying* was going to be the operant term here. They had no armament that was going to matter at all to a *Delta*, even before the retrofit of its armor: they were research vehicles, with nothing more than harpoons, corers and clawed manipulating arms meant for delicate bottom work. Now they buzzed around the *Delta* like angry wasps, but wasps without stings: and the *Delta* lay there, ignoring them –

– until one of them got too close to the huge bow and

began hammering on it with something. A rock, Nathan thought, held in its gripping claws –

Within seconds an E-plasma torpedo came searing out of one of the *Delta*'s tubes, burning its way through the water, and struck another of the surrounding craft, the biggest. It exploded in a starburst of electrostatic flame, and the pressure of the explosion rocked all the other little craft nearby, rupturing one, so that it cracked open like a dropped egg, shedding its air and its pilot into the water. The air lurched and bobbled upward in writhing globules; the pilot, crushed to death in an instant, drifted to the bottom with the rest of the flotsam from his destroyed vessel. The first small ship, the one which had had the temerity to attack the *Delta*, backed frantically away; so did the rest of its companions, those that were still intact, or had power left to move after the detonation ...

*

Inside the *Delta*, Marilyn Stark watched the little craft swarm furiously around her boat, and sat quiet in her Command chair, unconcerned. *That will have taught them to keep their distance, at least,* she thought, *and to respect superior force. After all, should I sit here and let them entertain themselves trying to claw us to death?* But that nuisance was ended for now. There was much more important business to tend to at the moment –

'It's back!' her sensor chief yelped, panic shrill in his voice. 'The *seaQuest* is back!'

She just smiled. *They're doing better than I thought they would,* she thought. *Not that it's going to do them any good. A last show of bravado: no more. Whoever's in that boat, he's a fine bluffer. But shortly it won't matter any more, to him or anyone else aboard her ...*

'*Captain!*' shouted Maxwell, not believing Stark's disinterest – then gulped at his own temerity, and shrank down in his seat. Stark just quirked that smile at him: she was really in too good a humor at the moment to chastise the poor creature. 'Relax,' she said to the Bridge at large, 'all of you. You're looking at a shark without teeth.'

Then she sat a bit straighter in her chair. *Extending a pleasure too far is vulgar,* Stark thought: *it's better to kill quick and clean than to toy with your prey.* 'Helm,' she said. 'Bring us around to zero-six-zero ...' She smiled slightly. 'Attack posture.'

*

Ortiz checked his readings, checked them again, and the altitude change told him the same thing both times. 'The *Delta*'s bringin' her barrels around on us!' he said.

Bridger stepped up beside him. 'Heading?'

'Zero-six-zero. She's movin' straight at us.'

Crocker looked at Bridger, the expression from the old days that said, *Head-to-head her?* Bridger nodded. Crocker instructed his helmsmen, and *seaQuest*'s bow swung around to match the *Delta* move for move.

'Chief O'Neill,' Nathan said, heading toward the Command chair, 'open up low band, all frequencies. I want everybody out there to hear me.'

'Aye, sir,' said O'Neill, and worked over his console for a moment. Bridger stopped by the Command chair, looked at it thoughtfully – and swung down into it. The Bridge got very quiet.

'Low band open, sir!' said O'Neill. 'Standing by for transmission.'

Bridger reached out to his command panel, cleared his throat, and hit a button there. 'Attention all colony craft and colonists. This is Nathan Bridger, commanding the Deep Submergence Vessel *seaQuest*, representing the United – the United Ocean –' His mind went blank. *Damn!* 'What the hell is it?' he whispered to Ford, who was now standing by him.

'United Earth/Oceans Organization.'

'– United Earth/Oceans Organization. We are here to protect and defend your facility. All craft free in the water, move to safe territory immediately. Repeat – move clear immediately ...'

*

And one of the very few things which could have startled her had now happened, so that Stark, even Stark, came up slowly out of her Command chair, with a look of utter astonishment on her face. 'Nathan Bridger ...' she said under her breath.

Maxwell came hurrying over to her, his eyes wide and frightened. 'Captain! Did you hear? *Bridger* is –'

'*Yes*, I heard,' she said, mildly annoyed: did he think she had suddenly gone deaf? All the same, Stark was bemused. The scuttlebutt had gone right around the Fleet and had come back the other way about how old Iron-Pants Bridger, right in the middle of building the most powerful submarine ever seen in the world's waters, had abruptly gone south in the brains and taken himself off to some desert island – and had there cut himself off from the world, like some kind of lunatic Prospero with an armful of computers, to do, if you please, *research*. Now Stark blinked, wondering what on earth had had the power to stir him out of his self-imposed solitude – for the word had gone around that he had refused numerous attempts to get him out of retirement again. 'I didn't think he'd ever come back ...'

Maxwell, though, knowing none of the man's history, was much more worried about other things. 'What's he doing here?'

'I don't know,' Stark said.

'And what if he's found the sabotage, and fixed it?'

Stark was busy considering the possible ramifications of this sudden appearance. 'Oh, I'm sure he found it,' she said absently. 'But he hasn't *fixed* anything. There's no way.'

Of that she was more than sure. That ship was one of the most complex, in terms of hardware, of any ship ever built: the old Space Shuttles were hardly more complicated. *seaQuest* had been made not to *need* much in the way of maintenance, and most of her most important systems were protected by way of redundancy rather than by having spares and extra parts on hand. Anything that broke had an identical system right behind it, and another after that, sometimes six or seven layers of redundancy deep: more than enough for even a very long cruise. There had been no protection for the ship, though, against her own systems' redundancy turning against her – which was a situation which Stark had carefully crafted and installed after she was relieved from command.

The concept had crossed her mind more than once while she was still in the center seat, all that while ago.

Stark had become determined that, while she was still in active service, no one else should command this ship without her permission – for so powerful a weapon was too important to be trusted in less talented, or faithful, hands than hers. Marilyn Stark had considered in some detail how to make herself, in essence, *seaQuest*'s guardian. Then, suddenly, after the Livingston Trench incident, Stark had found that she was going to have to begin to exercise that guardianship. Since she had spent so very long on the planning, it had taken her only a couple of weeks of work at the programming, and some clandestine installation work down in the bilge, to lay in the self-perpetuating virus routines that would prove to Fleet how big a mistake it had been to take a Stark out of the helm. The first time *seaQuest* saw action, she would fail disastrously – possibly even be destroyed. But Marilyn Stark thought not. She rather suspected that the ship would escape and crawl back to port. There would be any amount of uproar in the Naval hierarchy. And sooner or later the word would go out – no one else can handle this boat: get Stark. She would be recalled, and those who had relieved her of command would be disgraced, and she would quietly remove the viruses and then show the Navy once more how such a ship should be commanded –

Now, though, *that* scenario seemed to have come to pieces. As yet, she was more insulted than angry. That they should give her ship back to a lapsed officer, a beach-bum, a coward who ran away from his duty –!

'*Attention*, Delta-IV,' came the beach-bum's calm voice, '*I am prepared and willing to accept your immediate and unconditional surrender. Otherwise I will be forced to fire on you. You have twenty seconds in which to initiate your response . . .*'

Marilyn Stark settled back in her Command chair, and smiled.

*

Let's see if that *does anything*, Nathan thought, and closed the channel. 'Weapons control,' he said, 'flood all tubes, open all outer doors and bow caps.'

There was a shocked pause. 'But sir,' came the doubtful voice of Weapons Officer Phillips, 'only tube number one has anything in it!'

'I know that,' said Nathan. 'Just do it. Rack the shotgun; make the brave noise.' More to himself than to the rest of them, he said, 'We may not *be* tough – but we can damn sure *look* it ...'

*

'Sir, *seaQuest* has flooded all her torpedo tubes; outer doors are coming open.'

Stark rose from her chair and gazed levelly at her sensor chief. 'Well, now ... Any targeting sweeps detected?'

The man checked his panel. 'None,' he said, sounding wary, as if he thought this must be some kind of trick.

Stark shook her head and looked smugly over at Maxwell, smiling again as her certainty reasserted itself. 'Bridger used to drum it into us at the academy,' she said – 'the first thing you do before a torp launch is perform your targeting sweeps. If he's not targeting, he has no weapons. He's bluffing. The *seaQuest* is a sitting duck.'

She stepped forward, her heart swelling, for at last, at

long last, this was the moment of her revenge. After this, her life lay open before her: she could do anything ...

'Initiate fire sequence, Mr Maxwell,' she said softly. 'All six tubes.'

'But that'll take almost a minute.'

'I know.' Stark was dreamy-eyed as she watched the pictures forming in her mind. 'I want to blast her out of the water. It's time the student became the teacher ...'

THIRTEEN

'Okay, Weapons Control,' said Nathan. 'Talk to me ...'

Phillips's voice from the Weapons Control station sounded fairly bleak, as bleak as his own prospects. 'You've got your one E-plasma torpedo, sir – tube number one! I'm afraid that's all! And still no targeting!'

Ford looked up from his station. '*Delta* is settling into attack position!' he said. 'Getting ready to fire!'

Bridger sat there weighing his options. However little he liked them, there was nothing to do but exercise them.

He reached down and hit a switch on his control panel. 'Okay, my friend,' he said softly. 'You're on your way. Do the deed.' *And Godspeed ...*

Bridger glanced aside to one of the screens on the WSKRs panel, and craned his neck to see past Ortiz. Junior's screen showed what he was looking for: the starboard-controlled egress port, a tiny dimple on the dark exterior skin – small enough, in contrast to the rest of a thousand-foot hull, to miss if you didn't look very closely. A slim silvery shape flashed out through it at speed, its paleness broken toward the front of its body by the straps of a harness. *Darwin* ... Nathan thought. *Hunt* ...!

A few seconds later, O'Neill called out to him, 'Smaller craft have all retreated from the area, sir!'

That at least was a relief. Ortiz looked up as well. 'The renegade is targeting on us now, sir!'

Terrific, Nathan thought. *But better on us than the colonists – I guess*. 'Sir, our torpedo doors are open and ready to fire,' said Ford.

Nathan did nothing, said nothing; just waited. 'Captain,' Ford said urgently, 'our only chance is to fire first!'

Nathan would have grinned all over his face at the sight of his Ex-O trying to teach his grandpa how to suck eggs – except that he was waiting for something, and didn't dare breathe, hardly dared think, until it happened. He held up his hand to keep Ford quiet for just a little longer, then leaned forward in the Command chair, and swallowed, waiting –

'*Delta-IV* is flooding *all* her torpedo tubes!'

Nathan glanced at Ortiz. 'All her tubes? You sure?'

'Yes, sir. Six tubes. The bow caps are still closed – no ... Pressure equalization, bow caps cycling open *now* ...!'

Indeed, Loner, the foremost WSKR probe, was already quite close enough to the *Delta* to show this on its screens: the dark pits of the doors opening, and deep down in their throats, perfectly visible to the super-acute vision of the probe, lay the dully-glinting noses of the torpedoes, ready to fire. Nathan gazed at them, fascinated by the view, as a bird might be fascinated by a snake. He swallowed. *Don't let her rush you. Wait for the moment. Wait ...*

'She never did know when to quit,' Nathan muttered as he stared at the screens, and at the outline of the *Delta-IV* hanging there, black against the dimness. *It's meant to be*

complete, isn't it, he thought. *No chance of us making it home –*
any of us: especially not the innocents who saw you get the worst of
our last skirmish. Well, I have news for you. Yet at the same
time, he pitied Stark – plainly unable to cope with what
years of living on the edge of violence had made of her.
Her only remedy had been to dive wholly into it. Nathan
didn't flatter himself that his solution had been in any way
superior; but at least he hadn't killed anyone doing it.

Except Carol –

He shook that thought away. There was no point in
dwelling on it.

And maybe Darwin – 'Come on, now, come on, talk to
me ...!'

And on one of the screens, something silvery gleamed
against the darkness, something moving fast, striped with
the bands of a harness ...

Nathan leaned forward, watching, his heart genuinely
feeling as if it were in his throat: he could scarcely breathe,
and his heart hammered like native drums in some bad
old movie. Darwin was swimming swiftly along the under-
side of the *Delta*'s hull, heading for the ship's centerpoint.
Near his head, a tiny spark of flashing light paced him. It
was at that moment that the ship's size really registered on
Nathan for the first time: for Darwin was only five feet
long, and it was taking him a long time to get to the target
zone, much longer than he had thought. *Come on – come*
on, Darwin –!

The rest of them watched him too, frozen. Then there
was a sudden burst of speed, and Darwin was flashing
along, was almost there. He dropped out of Loner's sight,
just around the curve of the *Delta*'s bottom –

– and the view shifted to Junior's: the number three

WSKR had been drifting quietly downward all this while, too slowly to register, possibly, as anything but another bit of wreckage from the minisub the *Delta* had blown away. With his view they could all see Darwin slide right up against the *Delta*'s hull. Junior's view zoomed in on the dolphin's head as he turned and slapped the strap he held up against the renegade sub's hull. Something dark seemed to adhere there: the strap dangled, twisting in the current. Darwin twisted downward, turned, and swam back toward the *seaQuest* like lightning; and as he did, a small green flashing light came from the dark thing he had left on the *Delta*'s hull – and flashed again –

*

'Get us a bit closer,' said Marilyn Stark. 'I want to make sure we split her right in two –' Then her head snapped around with terrible suddenness as, all through her ship, a high, intense *pinging* noise rang out.

She spun around in her seat. '*WHAT THE HELL IS THAT?*' she cried. Her officers stared at her helplessly, and just as helplessly she stared back. Not at them, but at the hull-incursion indicator. Small mass, emitting radio as well as sound. The ping rang out again. And again …

'No,' Stark muttered, refusing to believe what the indicator was telling her. 'How could he do that …? He – he "*tagged*" us …!'

*

The ping echoed through *seaQuest* as well, and Nathan was gladder to hear it than he ever had been to hear a noise in his life. 'We have a targeting signal, Captain!' Hitchcock shouted in triumph. 'Hot and steady! Range, eight hundred twenty –'

Weapons Officer Phillips swung around from his control board, his face that of a man reprieved on the scaffold. 'Torpedo is *locked on target*, Captain!'

Bridger's jaw set hard, and all of a sudden he felt horribly sure that everything and everyone was spiralling down on him, waiting for one word. One command. He gave it.

'Fire ...!'

*

Stark flicked open the security panel of her command console and daintily pressed one long, slim finger down on the firing switch. The six confirmation lights came on – but instead of the steady glow of a launch they were flashing, blinking small simultaneous red eyes at her, defying her to do anything about it. She hit the firing switch again, mashing her thumb down on it, once more, and again – and still nothing happened but the blink, blink, blink ... *Failed,* she thought, *machinery failing me as men have failed me, it's not fair, it can't be happening –! Not now!* As her mouth twisted into a snarl, she swung around and bent all her baleful regard on Maxwell. 'Why aren't we firing, dammit?!'

'Our tube doors aren't locked open, Captain!' he said desperately. 'Launching sequence will be ready in ... another eight seconds!'

But the pinging went on without a break, and Stark could already hear the upscaling whine of a torpedo. Whether it was real or just inside her own head, it didn't matter. When her own sensor chief turned towards her with a face as white as salt, she knew which was the truth. And still it didn't matter. Not now. Not any more. Not ever ...

'*seaQuest* has fired! One torpedo – locked on target ... ninety meters now and closing ...!'

Marilyn Stark glanced at Maxwell, and her expression slumped into resignation. 'We haven't got eight seconds,' she said. 'We haven't any time at all.' She shook her head slowly, and showed her teeth in what might once have been a smile.

'Bridger ...'

*

Junior's view showed it more clearly than Bridger had ever seen it before, or had ever wanted to see it. The torpedo went barrelling in, shifting slightly as course corrections passed from its homing head to its control surfaces, until the *Delta* was blotting out everything else. Then, finally, the strike: the casing of the torpedo blasted apart under the impact and its own internal explosive charge unleashed the activate E-plasma charge. This burst out with terrible force, fastening like a hungry starfish against the *Delta*'s hull, sending tendrils of blinding blue-white energy crawling all over it, and even the twenty-percent charge it carried was too much for the elderly steel hull beneath the patchwork of retrofitted armor. The hull started to crack, peeling outward like the shell of an egg smashed from within, and all six torpedoes blasted uselessly from their tubes, spiralling away upward, uncontrolled and harmless.

Slowly, slowly, the *Delta* began drifting downward, the cracks radiating wider and wider through her hull, any remaining helm control now completely gone, her inertia still carrying her gently forward, toward one of the huge jagged rifts in the undersea prairie, then slowly, slowly, down and into it. It was odd how something so massive, so ponderous, could suddenly seem so ephemeral, like a feather, drifting down into the dimness, into the blackness of the rift, even blacker than she.

The three WSKRs passed by and hovered over the trench. First Loner, then Mother, went down after the sinking ship. Behind them, Junior hesitated only a moment, hanging above the edge of the rift, sorting conflicting signal traces. Then, as if the probe had made up its mind to discard some small target for a much bigger one, it hurried down after the others.

*

seaQuest's Bridge was in pandemonium: the crew cheering, laughing with relief, shaking hands.

In the Command seat, Bridger sat and gazed forward for a few long moments, thinking – or trying not to. Presently he glanced down at his hand on the switch: quite steady, as if the control on which it rested was nothing more important than a light switch.

Ford had come quietly up beside him. 'Where's Darwin?' Nathan said, his mouth still dry.

'Back aboard five minutes ago,' Ford said. 'Westphalen's down getting the rebreather off him.'

Nathan nodded, not moving. Ford looked down at the hand which still rested on the switch, still rock steady. 'I guess you never lose it, sir ...'

Nathan shook his head sorrowfully. 'No,' he said, his

voice full of regret, a voice haunted by the past inevitably come home to roost. 'No, I guess you never do ...'

*

Nathan saw to the stabilization of the situation: the WSKRs deployed to keep an eye on things, crews sent out via TeamCraft to help the people at the research station repair any damage, and to help them recover their dead; other TeamCraft sent out to examine the wreckage of the *Delta* for any possible survivors.

Then Nathan headed out to have a look around his ship, to see how the continuing repairs were going, and to see that people were all right after the attack. Practically the first thing he saw down the port passageway was a group of military crew walking past a couple of science crew, and eyeing them warily, as if they might go off. *So much for us all becoming fast friends after our great trial together,* Nathan thought as the military crew approached him. *A lot of work to do yet ...*

As the three military crew passed Bridger, they saluted. 'Hello, sir,' one said, and 'Good job today, sir ...' said another. They held salute.

Nathan just nodded at them and kept going, letting them take it as they would. It was going to take a lot of work for him, too, to get used to the formalities of the service again. A lot of old habits to break, for if you chose to be in a service, you had to agree to be in it without subverting it ...

... much.

Nathan grinned and went on his way: further down the passageway, then down a stair, making for the sea deck.

Halfway down the stairs he spotted Ford coming along the hall toward him, apparently looking for him. 'Excuse me, sir –'

Nathan finished coming down the stairs, and they fell in together as Nathan headed down the hall. 'The recon party has just returned from the downed *Delta*. They have survivors with them.'

Bridger thought a moment. 'Secure one of the aft compartments – set it up as a makeshift brig until we get back to Pearl.' He paused, then said, '... Stark?'

Ford shook his head. '... But according to the recon party,' he said, 'she wasn't among the casualties, either.'

Somehow this struck Nathan as no particular surprise. 'Was the *Delta*'s mini-sub in its bay?'

Ford looked at the electronic clipboard he was carrying, to see if the information there had been newly-updated. 'None reported, sir. – You think maybe she ...?'

Nathan thought about that a moment, then shrugged. Right now it made little difference: though he had to think, at least briefly, about what Marilyn Stark would be like after this if she had lived. Would a defeat like this break her? Or would it make her more determined than ever to get back what was her own ... or what she considered her own? *A little nightmare,* he thought, *to follow you around and haunt your nights when they get too quiet. The sea is big, and dark, and there are a lot of places to hide and lick your wounds and recoup your forces. She did it once. She could do it again ...*

They walked along without saying anything for a few moments, watching the crew tidy up, looking into the occasional open doorway as they passed it. 'Sir ...' Ford said then.

Nathan looked at him as they walked. 'The crew is very

194

proud of what you did today,' said Ford. 'It was quite a thrill ... for *all* of us ... to see the old Nathan Bridger in action ...'

Nathan nodded. Feeling more than slightly melancholy, he said, 'That *is* who you saw today, Commander. That's exactly who you saw ...'

But why should I be so unnerved by it? he thought. *Thrown back into the ship I created, the position I longed for, worked night and day for ... then walked away from, thinking I'd never see it anyway. And then found I had been deluding myself. Poor Nathan, to be given your heart's desire –*

'Sir,' Ford said. Nathan looked up in some surprise, thinking that the somber tone of his voice should have been enough to send most people on their way: but Ford plainly had other things on his mind just now. He hesitated: this was costing him some effort. 'Captain, I –'

Nathan let him take his time. 'I want to apologize for not being honest with you,' Ford said. 'It was wrong, and I regret it. I was just –'

'Following orders?' Bridger said, gently ironic.

Ford looked at him. 'Yes, sir.'

'Well, I guess somebody has to ... Just remember after this that before you use your weapons, you should try using your head ...'

'Yes, sir.'

Nathan sighed, then. 'Once the recon party is squared away, let's get underway for Pearl.'

'Would the Captain like to take the helm?' Ford said.

'I'm sure you can handle it, Commander,' Nathan said.

'Aye, sir ...' And Ford went off to see about it.

Nathan went on making his way down to the sea deck.

In the pool there, Darwin was swimming lazy circles, upside down half the time. A fish hit the water near him: a mackerel. He snapped it up without stopping. 'Thank you!' he said.

'I should be thanking *you*,' Nathan said from where he sat at the edge of the pool. 'You risked your life today. For me. For this ship.'

Darwin came about from the upside-down position to look at Nathan rightways as he passed in the latest circle. '*Like* – "this ship",' he said.

'You do?'

'Yes,' Darwin said, sounding rather surprised that Nathan needed to ask. 'Comfortable. Many things ... fascinating. Things to *do*. We stay here ... a while?'

Nathan sat there, staring at the mackerel he was holding. It stared back, not very expressively. When he looked up again, Darwin was beside him, resting his head on the coping, looking at Nathan, waiting.

'I don't know,' Nathan said. 'Here –'

He offered Darwin the fish. Darwin took it, swallowed it whole, and leaned there, looking at Nathan.

Waiting ...

*

It was dim in his quarters. The little frame gleamed dully gold in the soft light as Nathan pulled the photograph out of it, trying just for the moment to study it objectively, as if it were a picture of a stranger. The photograph was of a woman in her forties, wearing a cotton sundress, smiling, her golden hair blown back by some breeze: the face serene, happy.

Slowly Nathan moved over to the imaging port of the computer and slipped the picture down onto the glass plate there: then touched his password in at the console. The lights dimmed further –

The hologram swirled and formed again, and suddenly, there she stood: still, almost caught between one breath and another, caught in the flush of life and joy. He moved toward her, almost unable to breathe at the sight. If she should move, if she should speak –

He reached out to her hand.

His hand went through it . . .

Nathan breathed out, then: went to a chair nearby, and sat down, looking at the image. Even if it should just seem to breathe –

'I've been workin' on a motion device,' said a voice from behind him.

Nathan looked over his shoulder. Lucas was standing there.

'I haven't been able to nail down the mechanics yet,' Lucas said. He sounded very subdued, looking at Bridger: Nathan wondered exactly what it was in his expression that might be causing this . . . 'The door was open,' Lucas said.

Nathan nodded. Slowly Lucas came in, gazing at the image. 'She's pretty,' he said after a moment.

'Yeah,' Nathan said softly. 'She was.'

Lucas looked hesitant, twitchy. 'I just came by to tell you that I thought it was – effective – the way you handled the situation today.'

Nathan had to smile. '"Effective"? Thanks.'

There was an awkward pause.

'So,' Lucas said, 'you gonna stay, or what?'

197

Nathan was vaguely astonished. Why should he care, one way or another? More to the point, why was he having such trouble simply saying 'no' and sending the kid about his business? ...

'It's not that simple,' Nathan said.

'Why not? You like it here, don't you? I mean, this is *your* ship –!'

And so it was, heart and soul. Physical and real: much more physical than this image which the ship had made possible ... 'I made a promise to somebody,' Nathan said softly.

'Her?' Lucas said.

Nathan nodded. 'Her name was Carol,' he said.

Lucas stepped up beside him and, to Nathan's astonishment, sat down and looked at the image for what seemed a long while. Then, very quietly, he said, 'Were you two happy?'

Nathan was surprised at the seriousness of the question – even more surprised that Lucas was capable of being so serious. 'Yeah,' he said, the understatement of the century about his lover, his best friend, his wife of twenty years: 'we were.'

Lucas shook his head, disbelieving. 'My parents were never happy,' he said. 'I mean, they can't even stand to be in the same room with each other. They were always tearing each other up, making each other feel like crap. I remember wishing that they'd just get divorced and get it over with ...'

'Why didn't they?'

Lucas let out a sigh. 'They said when they got married, they made a promise to stay together forever.' He shook his head. 'I guess they didn't count on things changin' ...'

Nathan looked over at Lucas. *Out of the mouths of babes,* he thought. *Change – it comes for us all. Which is the better part of valor? To back away from new and dangerous things, invoking old promises? Or to remake the promises . . . and try to do better, be wiser, the next time? . . .*

Above them, the allcall loudspeaker said, 'Captain to the Bridge! Captain to the Bridge!'

Nathan sat where he was for a long moment, looking at the image of Carol. Beside him, Lucas looked at it too, wanting – who knew what?

But Nathan knew what he wanted . . . finally.

He stood up slowly, took a breath.

'You know,' he said, 'I think that's me.'

He headed for the door.

*

The Bridge was very quiet when he got there: only minimal crew were on post. Just after he crossed the threshold, the lights went abruptly dim.

Oh no, he thought. But Hitchcock was heading for the hatchway as he came in, and she saw his expression and smiled.

'Don't worry, Sir,' she said. 'It's the Night Canopy. We dim the lights six hours out of every twenty-four.'

'To give the crew a sense of night and day,' Nathan said, and nodded. 'Very good. Thank you, Commander.'

She nodded back. 'Good night, sir,' Hitchcock said, and went out.

Nathan wandered in, relishing the emptiness of it all, the peace, and paused there in the middle of the room, looking at the forward screens, the darkness of the sea.

Ford came up beside him and stood with him, silent a moment, gazing out into the dark. Then he said, 'We are in contact with UEO Command, sir. Admiral Noyce.' Ford paused, then said, 'He's asking if *Captain* Bridger is available.'

Nathan spent a moment more gazing at the dark sea: several moments. Then he turned to Ford.

'Yes, Commander,' he said. 'Tell him Captain Bridger is aboard.'

Ford smiled and moved off to his station. Bridger, for his own part, stepped over to the Command chair, looked at it for a moment: then slipped down into it, taking his place at last. He sat there a moment, then reached out to the link to communications, punched it.

'You and your goddamn licorice ice cream,' he said.

*

A shadow among the shadows, at depth, and at peace, *seaQuest* swept on toward Pearl and the oncoming morning.